NOT GRASS ALONE

NOT GRASS ALONE

Nelson Nye

Chivers Press • G.K. Hall & Co.
Bath, Avon, England • Thorndike, Maine USA

This Large Print edition is published by Chivers Press, England, and by G.K. Hall & Co., USA.

Published in 1996 in the U.K. by arrangement with the author.

Published in 1995 in the U.S. by arrangement with the Golden West Literary Agency

U.K. Hardcover ISBN 0–7451–2883–1 (Chivers Large Print)
U.S. Softcover   ISBN 0–7838–1384–8 (Nightingale Collection
                                                            Edition)

The text of this Large Print edition is unabridged.
Other aspects of the book may vary from the original edition.

Set in 16 pt. New Times Roman.

Printed in Great Britain on acid-free paper.

British Library Cataloguing in Publication Data available

Library of Congress Cataloging-in-Publication Data

Nye, Nelson C. (Nelson Coral), 1907–
   Not grass alone / Nelson Nye.
      p.   cm.
   ISBN 0–7838–1384–8 (lg. print: lsc)
   1. Large type books.   I. Title.
[PS3527.Y33N68   1995]
813′.54—dc20   95–11095

CHAPTER ONE

In the high passes the aspens were beginning to drop their leaves. The girl in the rattling stage involuntarily shivered as a blast of raw wind swooped down off the rimrocks filling the coach with the breath of winter. It was at least a change from the exhalations of the four other passengers, particularly the snoring Papago who, taking up most of her seat, kept jouncing around like a jug in a millrace.

Of the three men wedged in across from her the fat drummer in the middle appeared to be getting the most out of this ride, holding forth during the past several miles on everything from the vicissitudes of the coffee trade to the low price of cattle and current foolishness in women's hats. His tongue was about the nearest thing to perpetual motion Tara Drood had encountered. In the cramped confines it droned on and on with the maddening persistence of a bottled fly.

The man on his right, redheaded, with a face that was patchy with beard and rust freckles, presently broke in to say, 'You could hire out to Old Man Mike fer a windmill.'

The coffee salesman, reddening, reared back in affront and, half twisting around, looked about to explode. But nothing came out of him.

A saturnine amusement tugged the range rider's mouth as the expressionless eyes rested a moment on the girl. 'Crisp weather we're havin',' he said, touching his hat.

Tara said, 'Do you know Old Man Mike?'

'Who don't?' He grinned.

The third man spoke now. 'Cattleman, isn't he?'

'With three hundred thousand acres of grass you could call most anyone by that handle.'

The third man smiled. 'I'm with Crimp, Crane and Cranston—cattle buyer,' he said. 'Does he have any beef he'd like to unload?'

The redhead shrugged. 'Ever'body's got cattle. You don't hev to go to him. All these grangers comin' in, you could just about buy fer whatever you'd offer.'

The cattle buyer nodded. 'What I'm after is quality—the very best beef that money can buy.'

The rusty-faced cowpuncher appeared vaguely thoughtful. 'What'd you say your name was, mister?'

'Ames—Hollister Ames.'

'Yeah. St Looey, eh? Packin'-house people. That's a sizable outfit.'

'They've got money. Trouble is,' Ames grumbled, 'they don't want mixed lots. One big deal. Uniform grade—thirty carloads.'

Tara, listening, covertly continued her inspection of the personable buyer. A beautiful figure of a man he was, mature—probably into

2

his middle thirties, handsomely impressive in elegant silk tie, expensive clothes and congress gaiters. His mannerisms were both distinctive and charming, his hands seeming almost to speak for themselves. He had very white teeth, a neat black mustache, magnificent burnsides, and the liveliest eyes she had ever looked into.

They were approaching Stroud, and Tara desperately hoped the gorgeous gentleman was not planning to debark. Stroud was a cow town, trading center for the ragtail of small spreads clinging to the fringes of Star Circle's vast domain.

Suddenly afraid he might get off and that never again would she see his like, Tara sought for some way to keep him aboard, at least until they reached More Oaks for which she was bound on Jesusita's orders to fetch back the doctor for her grandfather.

She'd been looking forward to what time she might spend there. Reservation headquarters was a 'foreign' place filled, in Tara's head, with all manner of exciting enticements, perhaps even including an awful glimpse of the 'iron horse' that spouted smoke and—according to her grandfather's cowboys—made more noise than a convention of coyotes. A hell-tearin' community had grown up about the Agency— 'more wicked than Gomorrah,' if one could believe a quarter of the tales.

It was in Tara's mind to search out every crack of it. In her seventeen years she had never been farther from home than this miserable Stroud. And wouldn't be now if there had been anyone else for Jesusita to send. All hands— even the cook, were off on fall roundup.

Tara hated Stroud. It was here she had gotten her three years of schooling, despised and despising, forced to conform, penned up in her shell by the calculated cruelties and sneers of youngsters who hadn't been visited with the misfortune of having a half-Indian half-Mexican mother. They'd been jealous, of course—resentful of Tara's wild beauty and connections.

She looked again at Ames, something creeping over her, an exhilarating warmth she didn't attempt to probe or question. There was nothing like Ames around Stroud—she knew that much.

All the same he was a man, and men, she had found by a series of cautious experiments, had a great variety of weaknesses; they were all a little vain. She believed if she put her mind to it the interesting Ames could be kept aboard all the way to the Reservation. She got the handkerchief out of her pocket, and when he wasn't looking tumbled it onto the floor.

'Well,' the cowboy was saying, 'you've gone by your stop if you figured to auger at Old Man Mike. That was his gate the young lady got on at.'

The cattle buyer's look tipped around. The girl, as though unaware of his inspection, glanced out the window.

They were coming into Stroud, the driver touching up his teams as they wheeled with the dust between disjointed plank walks flanked by false-fronted buildings. Tara knew when the St Louis man spied her kerchief, and settled back with her eyes closed.

Ames took a look at her. Fingered his cravat.

She had good features, a face Cézanne might have roughed in while considering something else. Blunt, ungiving lines for nose and jaw, bitter-sweet mouth of earthy reds, sensual, provocative, too wide for the cheeks, too thin, too knowing in one so young—and she *was* young, devilishly so, to Ames' thinking.

He remembered her eyes, demurely closed now, and some far caution told him to leave this alone. Then the eyes came open, a suggestion of sly mockery gleaming out of their depths.

'Pardon me, miss...' Ames said, leaning forward, and when her look came round, held out the kerchief. 'Isn't this yours?'

She showed a pretty confusion, searching her lap, eyes afterward lifting. 'Thank you,' she said, stuffing it into her pocket.

That look gave Ames pause. He had always been a careful man, his adventurings circumscribed by an innate caution which, up until now, anyway, had kept him reasonably unscathed. The girl's look brought reckless

5

thoughts into his head.

One hand came up to touch her tawny hair. The red lips smiled.

Ames hitched forward, the drummer and puncher at either side of him forgotten. 'How well,' he said, 'do you know Mike Drood?'

'I don't think he'd see you. He's down on his back. He don't even come to the table any more.'

The cattle buyer watched her, face expressionless now. The stage swayed on two wheels and lurched around a sharp corner. The snoring Papago woke up and grunted. 'How well do you know him?' Ames persisted.

Her chin lifted willfully, unmistakably proud. 'Mike Drood is my grandfather.'

The stage pulled up with a screech of brakes in front of the Lone Star Hotel. 'Five minutes!' yelled the whip, and climbed down with the mail.

CHAPTER TWO

The Papago pulled himself together and got off.

The men wedged into the forward seat stiffly sat in a thickening silence. The drummer, after a couple of tries, with a surly impatience lurched onto his feet, this shift jiggling the coach on its braces. He said: 'Can I help you, miss?'

'I'm going on to More Oaks.'

The drummer, disappointed, clutched his hat and climbed out. Hollister Ames, stretching gratefully, squirmed into the vacated corner. 'As it happens'—he smiled—'I'm going there myself.'

The rusty-faced cowboy got off without remark.

The driver reappeared with a limp mail sack which he stowed in the boot. He went up over the wheel, handing down the drummer's cases, tossing a warsack off the roof which the cowpuncher caught. 'Stage leavin' straightaway fer More Oaks, Safford, Fort Duncan, Lordsburg, Hermanas, Mimbres, Columbus an' El Paso—*Aboard!*'

The coach shook a little as he settled into his seat. The shotgun messenger came out of a saloon and climbed to the box. The girl shut her eyes. Still gripping his sack, the range hand looked back unreadably at Ames, then moved into the brightness of the Lone Star's veranda.

The driver kicked off the brakes, snaked out his whip. The teams lunged into their collars, the coach lurched ahead. Stroud was left in the dust of another departure.

So the Old Man was sick, Ames mused, closing his eyes—sick enough to have sent eighty miles for a sawbones.

Ames methodically went over all he knew about Star Circle, everything he could dig out of memory. If there had been a son, the feller must be gone or planted. If he were still about, Ames would have heard of him. He kept track of such things. Odd facts could sometimes be translated into cash.

He'd forgotten about Star Circle until that cowhand had brought Mike into the talk. All his life Ames had been hearing things about Mike Drood; you couldn't gas about cattle without Star Circle coming into it someplace. The brand or the man ... they'd carved an empire out of this country. Feller must be in his eighties, anyway.

What was the girl called? Sara? Mara? ... *Tara*—that was it! There'd been something about the mother, but Ames couldn't seem to lay hold of it. Three hundred thousand acres! Good round numbers. Something a man could get his choppers into.

He had intended going on to El Paso, and various things about this intention continued to peck and pick at him pretty near to Creek Crossing, which was the next change of horses. He kept peering through his lids at the girl. She was watching him too. It was this that finally decided him to put off his business at the border where possible profits stood at only a few hundreds. The stakes here were limited only by the amount of intestinal fortitude...

Christ! Ames said to himself. He could be neck deep in clover for the rest of his life.

He pushed out his legs and fully opened his

eyes. Tara smiled.

Ames said, 'What's the matter with him?'

The girl didn't know. 'Been dosing himself with mule medicine but he don't seem to get no better. He don't know I've gone—' She said impulsively, 'I'd *never* get off that ranch if it was left to him!'

'This the farthest you've ever been from home?'

'Oh, I've been to Chicago and K.C.,' Tara lied, 'but everyone's been there. Mike says travel is a waste of good money. He thinks Star Circle is the hub of the universe.'

Ames smiled politely. 'Does your father agree with him?'

'My father's dead. According to Mike he was a pretty triflin' sort. He got killed,' she said, 'by falling off a horse.'

A little chilled, the man looked out across the passing land. They were coming down to Creek Crossing with the sun, like always, shining bright as cut glass. All the cold buyer felt wasn't a product of this fall air, but with the thought of that grass at the back of his mind he tried to account for her seeming lack of compunction by the hard facts of environment and the probable roughness of her raising.

No getting around this being a man's world. It was strictly hell on horses and women—anybody'd tell you that, and they were right. Throw the size of Star Circle into the mixture and put a dominant caveman-type like Drood in the position of God to this whole forsaken stretch of country, and no one but a fool would ever look for anything different. It was understandable she might appear a little callous. Life with a contentious old bastard like Mike could hardly be conducive to the flowering of tender sentiments. He was one of the last of the cattle barons, an unyielding diehard, holdout from a granite age—an irreconcilable, rougher'n a cob.

These reflections did not entirely remove the doubts and uneasiness the girl had stirred up. Reminded of her grandfather's touchy temper and the iron-fisted intolerance he brought to every obstacle, Ames knew for sure a man would be putting his neck straight out, locking horns with an outfit like Star Circle.

But the ranch was there, the old man was sick, and Tara was ripe to try out her wings. A feller didn't get to ride every day with an heir to three hundred thousand acres of grass.

He said, as the coach drew up by the station: 'They'll be changing teams here and, such as it is, there'll be hot food waiting and nothing else this side of the mountain.' He pulled out his watch, a fine English hunting case. 'We're running twenty minutes behind right now. Be dark before we come into More Oaks.'

The coach shook and teetered as driver and messenger with watery eyes and red noses came down over the wheel. 'Grubpile!' the whip growled. 'Be here thirty minutes.'

Ames got out and held up an arm.

Tara let him help her, then held onto him a moment while she stamped circulation back into her wobbly half-numbed legs.

She was practically famished after forty-five miles on the coach's lumpy cushions. The cold, windy ride had whipped color into her cheeks and, as she glanced up at Ames, her ridiculous hat somewhat askew, she made a picture any man was bound to think about.

She stepped through the door he pushed open for her, following the guard and whip inside the station.

This public room had a bar at one side, and a long plank table flanked by tipped chairs. The table was set with heavy plates and eating tools. A woman with her sleeves rolled up came out of the back carrying two bowls filled with steaming food. 'Set right down an' wade in, folks. I'll fetch the java straightaway.'

Ames pushed Tara's chair in, taking one beside her. He passed the bowls. She was used to plain fare—a sight plainer than this, and applied herself with a diligence that left little encouragement to conversational talents.

Ames, for his part, was content to eat likewise, though this was pretty poor chuck by his standards. Two or three times he slanched glances at Tara. One of these looks she trapped head-on, funneling it back with such straight-faced appraisal he felt like a coyote caught in the chicken yard. When she grinned he felt

11

pretty silly. She was scarcely more than a child, frumpily dressed, all eyes and red mouth.

He resented the heady excitement she roused in him. He liked his women with meat on their bones, something to get hold of—sophisticated, smart. There'd been something in that urchin grin that graveled, almost mocked him. For two cents he'd go on to El Paso!

But he knew he wasn't going to.

The driver, wiping his mustache, went out to oversee the changing of the teams. The shotgun handler, a couple of minutes later, picking up his mug of coffee sauntered off into the kitchen where his voice was occasionally interrupted by the bantering tones of the station keeper's wife.

Tara, when she got through, pushed back her chair and, bending over, appeared to be fussing with one of her shoes.

It was hot in here, but it was more than heat from the potbellied stove which brought the shine of sweat out on Ames.

When they'd sat down, the girl had pulled off her fur-collared coat, dropping it over the back of her chair. Now, as she bent over, her loose blouse fell forward, and Ames craned his neck. She could hardly have missed knowing what he was staring at. She let him look, coolly watching, for perhaps a dozen heartbeats. Then she straightened, still considering him. She got up, picked up her coat, and moved

12

across to the stove, putting her back to it, tucking in stray wisps of her tawny hair.

All the breath inside Ames seemed hung up in his throat, congealing there, refusing either to come up or go down. His mouth was dry. He felt all of a sudden like a goddam fool.

A clock, ticking someplace, seemed unconscionably loud.

He said, when he dared trust his voice, 'You fixing to go straight back with the doc?'

Her eyes probed him, 'Probably.'

Ames had never in his life been maneuvered like this. He told himself she could go straight to hell, but what he kept seeing was the paleness of flesh behind those made-over clothes, and that raft of green acres.

When the stage pulled out they were both aboard, each ignoring the other; Ames, filled with unmanageable thoughts, sat stiffly upright in the center of the forward seat. The girl rode lumpily in a corner of the other.

No word was spoken for perhaps a quarter-hour beyond the next change of horses. The sun was well down, hanging scarcely a rope's throw above the distant darkening purples of the rock-ribbed Galiuros. The girl's cheeks, even in this gaudy light, were beginning to look blue under the ceaseless whip of the bitter winds.

Ames managed to unroll and fasten the canvas flaps. 'About another ten miles. All right if I smoke?'

'P-Please do.'

He considered her through this deeper gloom.

Bending forward he quit his seat, the lurch and sway of the rocking coach slamming him hard against her. He apologized. Reaching back of her head to extricate himself, he let his arm, when he settled back, fall across her shoulders.

He was prepared for a rebuke but she said nothing, huddling there, all drawn in upon herself, holding herself that way for the next several miles. Ames, smiling to himself, felt better about his prospects, his virility flattered by the meekness he read into her.

Let her worry. She ought to be scared after trying a stunt like she'd pulled at that change station. He realized now that it had been a desperate attempt on her part to catch his interest. Apparently the girl was starved for attention, a natural result of being raised as she'd been, shut away from everything out on that ranch. He recalled the lengths to which some girls would go to get away from their environment.

He felt freer now. Aggression was the male's prerogative; it was distasteful and disconcerting to find one's role usurped by a female. Ames, being a man who found it intolerable, was glad to know she wasn't like that. Now he could plan, lay out the fine points of his strategy, warmed and enthused, aroused to best efforts by the healing prospect of that ocean of grass.

He displayed his finesse with adroit circumspection, not crowding the girl—not even when, at last with a sigh, surrendering to his warmth and gentlemanly conduct, she settled against him, letting her head fall back on his shoulder. Not even by a squeeze did Ames take advantage of the situation. All he did was talk, helping her pass the uncomfortable miles with colorful tales of his life in far places, gay and sometimes laughable vignettes of dangerous, exciting times safely passed.

She was, of course, enchanted.

When, at ten after eight, the driver pulled up in a shuddering stop before the Drovers' Hotel in More Oaks, Ames, helping her out, could see she was loath to take leave of him. He collected their luggage from the mustached driver—she had only a small satchel that had seen better days—and stepped back out of the way of the ingoing mail.

'You'll be wanting to freshen up,' he said, escorting her into the lobby. 'If you'll let me,' he smiled, 'I'd like to take you to dinner, perhaps show you the town—or are you too tired for that?'

Her pretense of considering did not fool him.

'At least let's eat together,' he said. 'After that, if you want, I'll help you find the doc. This

15

is kind of a rough place for a young lady to be alone in ... When you're ready, come down. I'll be keeping an eye out.'

CHAPTER THREE

Tara asked the clerk within Ames' hearing about the chances for a bath. The fellow had given every evidence of finding the notion preposterous. Distastefully eyeing her clothes and red lips, he had thrown out his chest as though to flog up a storm when his choleric glance chanced to fall across the book. The change in his expression was ludicrous. It was difficult to metamorphose so insulting a look into something which might pass for an astonished delight, but the man did. 'Er ah—absolutely! Miz Drood, ma'am. Number Seventeen.' Unctuous good will fairly oozed from his tones as he got down a key. 'I'll send a boy with a tub and hot water straightaway. Here,' he exclaimed, hastening out from behind his counter, 'let me have that bag, ma'am! ... No trouble—not a bit of it! Pleasure to have you with us!'

Ames, amused, stared after him as the pair moved off up the narrow stairs. He was prepared, should the girl look back, to give her a wink and a grin, but she didn't.

Ames' lids came thoughtfully down as he

16

picked up the stub of graphite pencil and inscribed his name in the thumb-smeared book. Young, inexperienced, she certainly was, but there was something about this that gave Ames pause.

He stood there, frowning, turning it over, unaccountably disturbed. Perhaps it was that hardness he had sensed when she'd spoken about her father, the way she'd gone away from him just now with never a backward glance. A feeling of disquiet stayed uncomfortably with him behind his roseate thoughts of Old Mike's acres.

It was risky, of course. Tampering with an outfit the size of Star Circle could get a man killed. No one but a fool would lay out to tangle with a gent like Mike Drood; but there was the beauty of it. The old man was flat on his back in a bed. Time he was over it—if he ever did get up—Ames could present the old bastard with a fact accomplished. Let him roar.

Ames went out into the street. He stopped the first man he met and said, 'Where will I find the law in this place?'

'That'll be Tig Tolliver—town marshal. Might try the Aces Up... That's it over there.'

Ames said, 'Thanks,' and struck out for it.

When he came back he was in a better humor. Tara Drood was Mike's heir. Once they were hitched, what the hell could he do? He might cut her off, but not by God until he

17

got a lawyer! Ames figured himself smart enough to take care of that.

At the desk the clerk pushed a key out. Ames said, 'Where have you put me?'

'Sent your luggage up to Ten.'

'You can fetch it back.'

'What's the matter with Ten? You haven't even been up there!'

'I came with Miss Drood. I want a room adjoining hers.'

The clerk's stare widened. 'I'm...' He said, cornered, 'Do you know who she *is*?'

'Ought to. I'm engaged to her.'

The clerk said limply, 'Take Eighteen,' and got the key for him. 'Soon's the boy comes back I'll send around your valises.' He watched Ames all the way up the stairs.

Closing his door Ames put the man out of his mind. The fellow might have his doubts, but he would hardly be likely to carry the thing further.

Ames could hear Tara splashing.

He shrugged off his coat, dropped his vest on top of it. Getting out of his shirt, he picked up the crockery pitcher and poured the cracked basin half full of water. The boy came with his bags. Ames, tipping handsomely, elbowed the door shut.

Getting out a spare shirt, he went back to the basin. He pulled a razor over his cheeks, and put on the clean shirt and a string tie. Beyond the thin wall the girl was still splashing.

18

Ames, grinning, shook his head. She had spunk, all right. He wished there was a little more of her. He got to thinking about the grass and the old man who owned it and the things that could happen if the old son of a bitch wasn't flat on his back.

He got into his vest and ran a comb through his hair. He put a cigar in his mouth and, frowning, fired up.

The mother was a breed—part red Indian, part Mex. Be an old crone by this time, wrinkled as a prune, or gone completely to fat like an overstuffed dog.

He had a brief thought about the ironies of achievement, of strength breeding weakness, the history of nine out of ten of these great pushers. No different out here than it was back east—clean back to the Romans. One generation piled it up; the next got rid of it. Imagine—Old Man Mike's kid marrying a mongrel.

'Christ!' Ames said softly. 'The old bastard must have been petrified.'

He picked up his fine coat and got into it, examining his reflection in the distortions of the mirror. Thirty-eight next month, and some of those years were beginning to pull at him. If a man didn't make it by the time he was forty...

Ames through practice had become quite accomplished at closing away things he didn't wish to think about. There was power in the mind, but a man had to know where he wanted to go.

This was the big chance, the coup he'd been waiting for.

Tara was the key. Eyes big as teacups. Paint on her mouth. Spindling body hardly thicker than a buggy whip. Ignorant, credulous, full of hell and vinegar—and reaching right out for it.

*   *   *

On her side of the wall Tara, briskly drying herself, stepped out of the tub. She lifted the mirror down off its nail and, standing it on end, backed away from it thoughtfully.

She knew what she looked like, but she had to take stock and evaluate what she saw in the light of what a man might be able to find in other girls. Regarding herself, she was filled with concern. The legs were too long, snake-hipped, almost boyish. Her chest stuck out like two knots on a stick.

She twisted, considering a variety of angles. Where had she been when the behinds were passed out? If a woman couldn't do no better than this, she'd better keep herself covered and do her sparking in the dark! She peered again with disgust at the coral-tipped pear-shaped mounds on her chest, the lean flanks, childish belly, that mop of tawny hair.

She considered the eyes. Not green, not truly gray. Expressive—really, she decided, her best

20

asset. The nose was too straight, the jawline too firm. Her mouth, when she reddened it, seemed faintly exciting ... She wondered if *he* thought so? She had a number of expressions she'd tried with some success, and she practiced these now, tailoring them for Ames.

What was he really like behind his pretty words and ways?

'Mrs Hollister Ames.' She said the name aloud, and grinned. Catchy—real class. She had a glimpse of Old Mike hearing it for the first time, and some of the color went out of her cheeks. Then her eyes turned resentful. It was a cinch she would never meet Ames' like again.

It just wasn't fair. Penned up on that ranch like a goddam heifer!

Steps sounded outside. There was a pounding on the door and Tara was half across the room before she stopped with a gasp, remembering her nakedness.

'Who—what do you want?'

'Tommy, ma'am. I come for the tub.'

'You'll have to come back.'

She heard his step on the stairs.

She frowned at the flour-sack drawers and made-over dress Jesusita had fixed for her. It was like a history of her life. Like all of her tomorrows if she didn't seize this chance.

She got into the things, seething with rebellion.

The poorest families in Stroud dressed their daughters better than this—and her a Drood, heiress to all those unplowed acres. All that money, and what the hell good was it? She didn't even have the price of this room. She had a dollar to eat on and nothing else but the return half of her ticket. 'You come straight back,' Jesusita had told her; if for any reason this wasn't practical, she was to put up with the Agent's family.

Tara tossed her head. For this little while she could do as she pleased. She could charge the room to Star Circle! She sat, puckered with thought. Why in the world shouldn't she charge up some clothes? That general store was still open, or it had been ... There must be a back way out of this place.

She jumped up with bold decision.

*   *   *

Ames was in the lobby, smoking, when she came down an hour later. She saw his eyes when the sound of her heels pulled his glance toward the stairs. Tara could hardly hold back her grin. She was almighty proud of herself in this get-up.

Ames got out of his chair and came forward, taking her in. He bent over his hat in a bow intended as tribute to her finery, and the clerk's eyes bulged. She was suddenly glad she had risked Mike's displeasure.

'Well!' Ames exclaimed, his glance roving over her. 'This was certainly worth waiting

22

for.'

She basked in his approval. Glorying in this moment, she took in a deep breath to make the most of her bosom, and came down the last stairs to take his arm with a lift of her head that was almost regal.

Gad! Ames thought, half strangled in her perfumery. She had gone to a great deal of trouble to impress him—had even put her hair up. Not her fault some bounder had sold her the trappings of a whore. She even had a beauty spot!

Ignoring the clerk, he ushered her grandly into the dining room. The place was practically deserted now, with only a handful of garrulous townsmen still hovering over their coffee and cigars, laughing at the jokes of an inebriated drummer.

Ames, with his back unbending as gun steel, toured her across the full expanse of the room, selecting a table as far removed as possible from the twist of heads and speculative glances. Lifting a chair with an elegant flourish, he seated her in such a manner that his own position, taken directly across from her, commanded all approaches, including any overtures likely to be inspired by the oxblood gown, plumed hat, or plunging neckline.

Consideration for the girl had little part in this arrangement. It was born of Ames' regard for the explosive possibilities. He had no desire to be confronted with anything which, in his

23

role of Tara's escort, might require that he show affront.

Two at the drummer's table appeared to have had more at the bar than was good for them. One was young enough to be reckless. Ames' eyes warned he would stand for no invasion of privacy. But the goddam farmer was getting up anyway.

One or two companions reached half-heartedly to stop him, but the fellow shook them off. Some remark fetched reluctant laughs as he quit the table and set out at a rolling walk to cross the room.

Tara, sensing trouble, searched Ames' face. 'What is it?'

She was smart enough not to turn and Ames, resettling his weight, let go of his breath in a gusty 'Nothing!' as the fellow, near enough to catch the glint of Ames' eyes, sheered away to go off in a hunt for the water closet.

Laughter laced with relief and contempt came out of the watching men at his table as the gimpy legged granger stumbled through a far door. The drummer, winking at Ames, embarked on another story.

The waitress looked nervous. 'Two complete dinners,' Ames said.

The waitress smiled, ignoring his painted trollop. 'Chicken or beef?'

'Chicken. With all the fixin's.'

Tara smiled too, looking around as the flatfooted hasher flapped off toward the

24

kitchen.

The granger, at this moment coming out of the toilet, caught that flash of red lips, and weaved toward them.

Ames turned still, every muscle frozen. If the fellow wasn't drunk, he was powerfully close to it, probably close enough to be thickheaded and nasty.

He careened against one of the tables, dragging off the cloth, but on he came, foolish-faced, floundering, recovering, making rough work of it. The men at his table became quiet again, watching with a kind of breathless avidity that was all the warning Ames needed. The man was going to make trouble.

Then, plainly cuing him, the drummer said clearly across that hush, 'Two will get you four Joe makes a monkey of that feller.'

The fool kept coming. He was like some dumb bull. The next table he came up against went over with a crash. He didn't even look around. He kept his eyes on that red dress and the girl who so outrageously, provocatively filled it.

'That's far enough!' Ames cried at him.

The fellow's stare never wavered. His feet, yawing somewhat, fetched him on, lurching like a freighter. He was flushed, still vacuously grinning, overalled under an open coat, with gray lumps for hands, and generally put together with the bulges of a hoof shaper.

Tara's face paled as he stopped beside her.

25

Ames was pale himself. It had been a mistake to come here. It wasn't fear of the man that was holding him rigid but fear for his plans. Fear of offending the girl, of losing her regard, pushed him onto his feet, where he said, coldly furious, 'Get away from this table.'

The man's head came around. The glassy eyes stared unwinking. He pushed out a big hand.

That was when Ames hit him square and fast upon the chin. It was a neat, well-aimed, short-armed stroke with the speed of a piston, but it hardly appeared to have the force to do what it accomplished.

The fellow's head went back, the whole length of him going with it in a foot-dragging stumble that deposited him spread-eagled on the floor ten feet away. He lay completely motionless for perhaps half a minute before he could twist on his arm and turn his head enough to find Ames. His eyes looked out of focus, but he finally got up. He stood staring, feeling his jaw.

'The young lady,' Ames said, 'is waiting for your apology.'

The fellow twisted for another look that took in her clothes and painted lips. 'Powerful young,' he mumbled, 'but a hoor's a hoor, and Joe Wheeler, by God—'

He left it right there and came in swinging. Ames ducked, trying to back clear. He wasn't quite spry enough. One of those maul

26

caroming off his cheek almost took an ear along. Flung into a dizzying spin, Ames fetched up on the wall, but shoved himself free before Wheeler could nail him.

Ames was shaken. He'd felt the power in those hands. It was going to take more than brass knucks. The man had the reach and he sure had the weight. But the rotgut sloshing inside him was no help. The next time—wide open—he came wading in, Ames stood as though petrified and let the man swing.

On flexing knees Ames let it fly over him. He came up with a pocket pistol wrapped in his fist and clobbered the man alongside the head with it.

Wheeler went down. He stayed down. The bunch at his table were all on their feet.

Ames put a stare like ground glass on the drummer. 'Pick him up and get him out of here.'

Some of the men slanched hard looks at Ames, but no one, apparently, wanted to argue with that pistol. The drummer and another man picked Wheeler up. Ames put the gun away, but the heat of his glance touched every face. 'Next one,' Ames said, 'may not be so damned lucky.'

CHAPTER FOUR

Tara could have eaten horse and never know the difference.

She was too filled with the seething whirl of her thoughts, with nervous excitement and the business with Wheeler, to know if she were crying or laughing. Her mind was confused, a jumble of impressions too bewildering and fragmentary for grasping and sorting. The nuances were there, significant but elusive in the sound of that fellow's hateful words, but over and beyond their searing sting glowed the shimmery vision of Ames springing up—an avenging Galahad straight out of the book!

The fact that Ames wasn't saying much escaped her. She was prattling along at a great rate, most of it forgotten as quickly as said. It never occurred to her that Wheeler's friends, or the granger himself, might be hatching ways to get even.

It had occurred to Ames. Common sense assured him that bunch would sniff round to find out who the girl was. The West would stand for a great many things, but the name of a decent woman was inviolate. Wheeler had taken her for a whore, but surely some of that crew would want to make sure.

This did not, however, draw the chill from Ames' stomach.

The town was crammed with masterless men, cheated farmers, drifters—all manner of riffraff, toughs run out of more settled communities. The Law was only one man, and Ames had already met him.

No telling which way those bastards would jump. Ames had told the girl he would show her the town, but only a chump would go out on those streets.

When the girl was done, Ames pushed back from the table. His grin drew an answering smile when he stepped around and took hold of her chair.

Getting up, she slipped an arm inside his elbow as coolly and naturally as though she'd been doing it every day.

Ames, marveling, was the more disquieted. He felt as if he were dreaming. Wasn't it, all of this, larger than life?

And yet she wasn't the first he'd enchanted. Charm was his stock in trade; he was practiced in maneuvering gullible women. Why should this one be any different? Maybe it wasn't the girl herself, but the old man, Star Circle, that inspired this disquiet.

He considered her out of the corners of his eyes. Impressionable. Ignorant. It was this Wheeler that was turning him so edgy. A really smart jill would have seen through Ames slick as looking through a window. He'd come up against a few; they'd acted like he was dirt.

This kid wasn't bad, not the way she'd have

29

him think; just putting on. Any fool could s
she was excited. Young, full of notion
trapped out in that cactus with a bunch
dumb brush poppers! She was ripe for th
business.

Ames was glad to find none of Wheeler
friends around the lobby. Tara said, 'I'll hav
to fetch my coat.'

'I'll go up with you. That wind's got th
smell of snow in it.'

She squeezed his arm, tilting back her hea
Warmth came out of her, curling around hin
real as the pressure of her fingers.

Here, Tara was thinking, was her chance t
escape, to get away from her aloneness and th
hateful things of home.

Ames saw the curving spread of red lips a
another of her silly posturings.

It graveled him to find that just being ne;
her seemed so disturbing. She wasn't eve
pretty!

Ames scoffed at himself, following her u
the skreaky stairs. It was her eyes that got you
He had never seen their like.

She was waiting for him, coatless, ju;
outside her opened door. 'Maybe it's to
cold . . .' She held herself motionless, watchin
him through the sheen of her lashes. Ame
stood, the victim of confusion, while she poke
at her hair, looking nervously away.

'Don't you think,' she said, glance swivelin
back at him, 'it would be more . . . I mean, ju;

the two of us?'

'You—You don't want to see the town?'

That sounded silly. Ames felt like a chump.

She poked out a slim foot. 'Maybe we could look around tomorrow...' Ames looked at her numbly.

Her upper lip pushed into a smile above the pink edge of a moistening tongue while her glance continued to poke and pry at him. 'I must have taken a chill on that stage. I can't seem to get warm—doesn't it feel cold to you?' When he still didn't speak, she said, a little impatient, 'I don't believe I ought to be out again in that wind.'

Ames didn't like it. There was certainly plenty of wind outside, but he couldn't help thinking she was making it too easy. He didn't understand, and the things a man can't get through his head frequently appear almighty suspicious. He uncomfortably suspected he was being maneuvered.

Ah, the hell with it! he thought, remembering the grass, all those unplowed acres. Once they were hers he could move onto Easy Street. This was no time to be squeamish. All that stood right now between himself and those acres was a damfool kid who couldn't get out of her woman's drawers quick enough.

Seeing it that way, the deal looked better. She ached to grab hold of life by the forelock. Nothing strange there, stuck out on that ranch seeing nothing everyday but the same old tired

31

faces. All he had to do...

If he didn't, someone else would.

Ames, pulling himself together, said a quick goodbye to caution.

'I expect,' he grinned, 'we could have a little party...long as we don't get too noisy about it. Here—' he put his key in her hand, 'my room's larger. Go on in while I nip down and rustle a little refreshment. Nothing like a bottle to chase away a chill.'

CHAPTER FIVE

Tara, after he'd gone, stood irresolute and frightened with the key burning into the palm of her hand. All her life seemed to be clutched in that hand, all the emptiness, the loneliness and heart twist, all the grinding aches of despair.

She felt truly cold now, clamping her teeth to keep them from chattering, the damp shine of her glance fever bright in the dimness. She had the feeling of being at a crossroads, that whichever way she stepped there could be no turning back.

It was the gray ghost of Mike Drood that turned her knees so weak with shaking, but Mike didn't need her. Mike had never needed anyone.

The painted number, expanding and

contracting on the dark wood before her seemed weirdly to throb in its enlarging brightness, to grow until all else was swallowed. Involuntarily, Tara shivered, torn between an almost frantic urge toward flight and an inescapable conviction that all she had ever cried for would be found behind Ames' door.

Not even the snivelings of conscience could change this—and that's all they were, these feelings of guilt. 'The pulin's of mediocrity!' the old man would have snorted, his never failing answer to recurrent storms of protest.

Old Mike knew how to get his way.

Did he think she was going to slop hogs all her life? Chase his goddam cows till she dropped in her tracks? Look what staying there had done to her father! Regard for others had never stood in Mike's way. 'Tough!' He would grin. 'You can't build a ranch just by wavin' a snot rag!'

Tara lifted her chin. Ames would take care of her. Sure, Mike would beller. But he wouldn't cut her out. He had nobody else he could leave all that grass to. She was the last of his kin.

She put the key in the lock and threw open Ames' door.

He'd left a lamp burning. She pushed the door shut, looking around with a woman's curiosity. There were his bags, closed, of course, properly fastened, his cloak carefully

33

folded over the back of a chair.

She admired herself in the mirror; she had never owned a hat like this with a feather. So gorgeously wicked! She patted her hair. A tiny, scared grin crept over the red lips. She hoped he wouldn't be too rough. Wouldn't do this dress much good to get wrassled in.

She knew a feeling of panic. She hadn't gone very far with those cowpunchers, a few kisses, a little squeezing; with Old Mike in their heads she'd never had much trouble stopping them when it suited her. But she never had been shut up in a room with one.

She found it hard to catch her breath. Who would hear if she yelled? Would anyone care?

She forgot the hat, forgot her hair, stood stiffly listening for his return. But all she could hear was her heart flopping around.

She had a wild, breathless impulse to get straightaway out. She even took a nervous step, but was caught in her tracks by the thought of Star Circle, the drudgery of those interminable days. She saw the world that was waiting for Mrs Hollister Ames.

She drew a cautious breath.

It wasn't as though Ames was somebody she didn't know. All those buffeting miles on the stage. A perfect gentleman. Important, handsome, a man who moved in the highest circles.

Ames was no saddle tramp.

She didn't know much about gentlemen

34

either, Ames being the first of that breed she'd bumped into. What difference did the size of the room make to sparking?

She listened, shaking, all her brashness turned to fiddle strings, but the steps went on past. Tara shuddered. Did all girls feel this way?

Cat-nervous, she jerked open the door.

Two rooms down, across the hall, a man's broad back came around and two eyes, calm as doves', considered her quietly. She had the weirdest feeling. She would have slammed the door but she was held there fast in that unwinking glance.

Filled with embarrassment, she watched him remove the shabby flat-crowned hat. He said, eyes twinkling, 'A windy evenin', Miz Drood.'

Why, he's an old man! she thought, observing the rumpled silvery hair. Then she gasped. *Miz Drood.* How in the world—

The man chuckled. He paused, seeming about to say more. Turning his key he looked over his shoulder. 'I hope,' he said, 'you'll be comfortable.'

The door closed behind him.

'Were you becoming impatient?' Ames said, startling Tara. 'I came as quickly as I could.' He held up a bottle. 'The best! It took some finding.'

She backed out of the entrance, making room for him.

He shut the door with a heel. His eyes looked

brighter and she was filled with confusion, wanting this, scared of it. *I hope you'll b comfortable.* She was suddenly furious. What right had that old fool to judge?

She sat on the edge of the bed, fiercely smiling, determined to show Ames she wasn afraid of him. He brought a pair of small glasses out of his pockets.

'Some people use branch water.' It was plai that Ames pitied them. You could tell h figured she had more sense. He set the glasses on the commode and filled them.

He brought one over. 'Try that,' he said, an held up the other. 'Your health, my dear. Ma we always know what we want ... and obtai it.'

He tossed his down in one gulp, watched smiling.

Tara emptied her glass.

She came onto her feet. Gagging, trying t catch her breath, she doubled over in a fit o uncontrollable coughing.

Vaguely she felt his hands on her comforting. Her throat was on fire all the wa to her belly. Her head whirled with sound bursts of dizzying color. When she got bacl enough breath and strength to get her face up Ames was helping her through a red fog to th bed.

She sank weakly down on the edge of it. 'It' a shame,' Ames said, patting her shoulder 'Stuff this smooth, I never saw it choke anyone

36

You must have swallowed wrong.'

She heard him cross the room and return. 'Drink this.'

She opened her eyes, then giddily, closed them.

A glass was pressed into her hand. She realized he was guiding it toward her face. She felt silly being such a damned bother, and was opening her mouth to oblige him and swallow when a whiff of the stuff made her suddenly shrink back. Before he could get it poured into her, she twisted her head away, pushing out with the glass and springing up as she did so.

Ames, smothering a curse, caught hold of her arms.

'I—I'm all right now.'

She opened her eyes. The left side of his coat was all darkening, dripping. She said aghast, 'I'm so sorry—'

'I ought to've had better sense.' He laughed, letting go of her. He poured water into the basin, wrung a towel out in it and vigorously dabbed at the spots. 'Guess I better get out of it.'

He came back in his shirtsleeves, ruefully smiling. 'You all right now?'

She bobbed her head.

Ames tipped up her chin. His face sort of floated. Lord, but he was handsome! 'I guess you know, Tara, honey, you're the most precious thing that ever happened to me. Tara, Tara ... it's a wonder I don't go straight up in smoke!'

Tara giggled. Wasn't he the caution! She fel
terribly proud and mixed up and wicked. H
said, taking hold of her, 'Where you been a
my life?'

Tara wished things weren't quite so fuzz
but when he pulled her against him, bendin
his head to find her mouth, she wouldn't hav
cared if the whole place fell in. She kissed hin
back in a delirium of passion.

It was just like kicking a hole through th
roof.

She could tell he was excited. He could tel
that she was, too.

Suddenly he scooped her up. Lord, but h
was strong! She snuggled closer, rememberin
the way he had handled that granger; thrille
with the feel of his mouth against hers
wondering, in a breathless incoherency o
delight, if he was really going to do it.

He put her down on the bed, then tool
another drink, gurgling it straight from th
upended bottle. But when he poured a
brimming glass for her, she pushed herself up
feet to the floor, peering at it dizzily, wonderin
if she dared.

She tasted the liquor, shuddering. Knowin,
he was watching, she tried another sip. It ha
more authority than those little yellow chillie
the Mexicans were so fond of. It was just lik
catching a hoof in the gut. But she got it down
She felt pretty set up.

Ames got onto the bed and dropped his head in her lap, flashing his teeth at her. He was a great one for grinning. She reckoned he sure knew a plenty about women. It kind of made her mad, and something stirred in some far jumble of her thoughts, but the room was so whirly she couldn't come up with it.

She reckoned she had better get off the bed, but Ames said, smiling up at her: 'Longest lashing I ever seen on a woman. Eyes like stars.' He captured a hand. 'Don't ever go away from me, Beautiful.'

He put his mouth against her dress, kissing her through it, playfully nibbling.

She got her hand away from him. She cuddled his face, brought her mouth down on his, keeping it there until the both of them, gasping, had to twist apart for air.

He sat up, then, hauling her against him. She felt his lips along the side of her throat, and one of her breasts was suddenly bare in his hand. She trembled, whimpering, beside herself almost, gasping and moaning in an ecstasy of fright and wickedness.

Ames could feel the craving in her. She pulled his head around, panting, but when his hand hotly came against a knee she lunged away. Wrenching free, she sprang up, wild and fierce as a panicked colt.

She whirled toward the door but he was there before her, brightly watchful. She heard the clatter of the key as he removed it. She could see the narrowing gleam of his teeth.

'Let me go! Let me out of here!'

He made to catch her, but she eluded his reach, backing away from him, step by step. She had, as she saw it, only one thing to bargain with, and the price of that was going to have to be marriage; in no other way would she be free of Star Circle.

He was breathing hard with the edge of that grin still hanging on his lips. 'Don't you know when a man gets started—'

'My grandfather's sick. I've got to get a doctor!'

'We'll hunt for one tomorrow.'

His continued advance kept forcing her back. She bumped against the bed, looking trapped and desperate. Ames stood watching, knowing he had her.

'I'll scream!' she cried.

'And will you say you're Tara Drood?'

'My name's in the book!'

Ames laughed. 'Go ahead.' His hand lashed out and caught her dress at the neck. A savage jerk ripped it down the front. He threw it back at her, grinning.

'Go on, sweetness. Yell.'

She whispered, frozen, 'They'll hang you for this.'

'Because you're Old Mike's granddaughter?'

She pulled the torn cloth up across her flesh.

'Nice girls,' Ames said, 'don't smell like distillery. They don't smear paint on their

40

mouths or wear parlorhouse clothes or get found in men's rooms. When they do, this country has another name for them. You want to guess what it is?'

CHAPTER SIX

She spent the night in Ames' room. Because she couldn't get out.

He'd been too shrewd to mark her. He hadn't attempted brute force—just kept eternally at her, heckling, grinning, putting his hands on her, trying to wear through the thin shield of her resistance. Two or three times he had mighty near done it when her own stirred-up feelings had almost betrayed her.

She guessed she had been pretty rightdown stubborn. She had held out for marriage, and come through the ordeal with her virginity still intact. She reckoned no victory was ever without some tag ends of worries.

Ames had looked at or handled almost every inch of her. She had learned a few things about them both in the process that didn't seem to drum up any great amount of comfort.

Shaking the hair back away from her features she stared at the thin edge of light above the sill. She thought it could have been a whole heap worse; at least Ames had been promoted into a promise of marriage. She had shoved a man between herself and Old Mike.

Now she was alone. Ames, locking her in, had gone off with the key. He'd said he'd be back, and that was all he had told her.

Cold gray dawn was marching over the hills. The wind was still blowing. Lord, but she felt achy!

She got up and stared in the wavy mirror. Her hair was a fright, and her face looked like she'd been hauled through a knothole—another of Mike's expressions. She was reminded she still hadn't got hold of the doctor. But after dosing himself for two weeks with mule medicine, another few hours of the stuff wouldn't kill him. Mike was too damned ornery to die anyway.

Lordy! Was he going to boil when she walked in with a husband!

She splashed water into the chipped basin and got out of the wreck of the gorgeous red dress. She found a towel Ames hadn't used and, wetting it, scrubbed herself. After bathing her face, she felt a little better. She washed herself clean down to the elastic of her new dollar drawers. She didn't dare to get out of them. Drying herself briskly, all shivery and goose bumps, she got rid of her slops and wiped out the bowl. She found Ames' comb and ran it through her tawny hair.

She found her hat in back of the bed and put it on, admiring the feather. She'd never seen one like it, so fluffed up and fluttery. About to

42

turn away, she discovered she still hadn't put on her dress.

She scowled at it, frowning. Without needle and thread there wasn't much she could do with that great gaping tear. And those wrinkles—Lordy!

She was still standing there when Ames opened the door.

With a gasp she started to snatch up the dress; then, glaring, ignored it.

Ames pushed the door to, coolly eyeing her. Grinning, he tossed down an armful of parcels. 'Get into those and get rid of that hat. I'll be in the dining room. Come down when you're ready.'

He caught up the red dress and, before she could stop him, slipped out and pulled the door shut. She listened to his steps tramping off down the hall. Heard the opening and closing of a window, then his steps coming back, going down the skreaky stairs.

She got the key, then closed and locked the door. Going over to the bed she tore open one of the bundles. It was a long full skirt, darkly gray, with a short, stylish jacket.

She could scarcely keep from shaking. It took her back to Christmas mornings when her father was still alive. That jacket! There was real horsehair in it—and those lavender buttons and muttonleg sleeves! With her heart pounding madly, she tore open the rest of the bundles.

Lordy, lordy!

A white starch-stiffened shirtwaist with snowy ruffles and a tiny gold watch pinned just in front of the left shoulder. City stockings and high-buttoned shoes with leather as soft as the feel of your face! A pillbox hat, the exact shade of the jacket buttons, with a dark band and a veil as sheer as a cobweb fastened onto the front in a kind of Mormon tangle.

Tara stared and stared and, with her eyes fiercely bright, passed the silk of the underthings through work-roughened fingers and tremblingly held them up to her cheeks. She cried a little before she began to get dressed.

She could hardly believe it was herself in such finery. The little jacket was tight and snug. She had a wonderful time trying the hat at various angles, then took it off reverently and put up her hair. With the hat on again, she stood off and eyed her reflection.

She looked terribly expensive.

*   *   *

Ames, in the dining room, threw aside his paper, and for the dozenth time consulted his hunting-case watch. What was she doing? Eight o'clock already! The place was filling up. Becoming suddenly aware of the twisting of heads, he canted his own, a little astonished in spite of himself.

Considering her critically, he grudgingly admitted it was hard to believe he was seeing the same girl. Those duds had cost him a pretty penny, but it was worth it! He'd never seen such a swath of dropped jaws. She looked the closest thing to regal these yokels had ever stared at—like a princess, Ames decided, thinking back to the time he'd seen one in St Louis. She stood there trying to find him, a little diffident but proud, perhaps for the first time conscious of her place as heir to all those unplowed acres.

Something about her seemed different. Her hair in this light was like newly churned butter, more of the gold showing through, less of the red ... He watched narrowly as she came toward him.

She'd left off the paint. But it wasn't that. Even her walk was somehow different. She was more assured, and he wondered if getting those clothes might in some fashion turn out to be a damned mistake.

He got up and held a chair for her. There was something almost gracious in her acceptance of this service. You might almost think she *was* a princess!

Ames seated himself with a disgruntled frown. Leaning over, she said in a kind of choked whisper, 'Oh, thank you!'

He felt a little reassured. After all, she was hardly more than a child, fairly bursting with pride over all this attention. 'My pleasure,' he

45

grunted, and turned to give their order, afterward settling back in more comfort.

He could handle her all right. He wished he could feel as sure of Old Mike. 'We'll get hitched,' he said, 'and then we'll hunt up the doc.'

The old man was sure going to raise the rafters. Crew was probably out on the range, else the girl wouldn't be here. Ames wasn't fooling himself. What he was up to could bring on a shooting if the old bastard wasn't plumb down on his back. He dragged his mind away from it. Time enough to cross that bridge when he got there.

He left a tip when they got up. Tara, taking his arm, stepped into the lobby, ignoring the heads wheeling around to stare after them. A different clerk was on the desk, and Ames inquired where they might find a preacher.

The clerk looked them over. 'You're in luck,' he said, grinning. 'One right in the house. Benton Pearce. Room Fifteen.'

'Is he in?'

'Ain't seen him come down yet.' The man eyed them curiously. 'You fixing to get hitched? Say, ain't you the feller—'

Ames, cutting him off, asked where a doctor might be found.

The man's interest deepened. 'Ain't but one. Old Blodgett—took off last night for the Twin Peaks country.' His glance cut to Tara. 'Somebody sick out to your place?'

Tara's fingers tightened. She said coolly, 'He'll get over it,' and moved toward the stairs.

Ames trailed after her, annoyed at the way news flew about this town. The clerk's smirk implied he guessed a lot more, and made it hard for Ames to walk off without hitting him.

But a heady satisfaction was swelling through Ames. Twin Peaks was a good forty miles to the north, a jaunt no sawbones would be taking for the hell of it. Time they caught up and steered him toward Star Circle, anything might happen. If Mike hadn't been pretty sick, Ames would never have met Tara.

Her eyes searched his face when he caught up with her on the landing. 'What are we going to do?'

'Hire a buggy, I reckon. We'll have to go after him—'

'I mean about the preacher.'

'I'll see if I can get him up.'

She was watching him. 'Any reason I shouldn't go with you?'

Ames took hold of her elbow. They climbed the rest of the stairs. Letting go of her then, Ames rapped on the door.

No response. Ames, more vigorously, knocked again. When still nothing came of it, Ames, stepping nearer, put an ear to the wood. He glanced at Tara. 'Nobody home.'

She said impatiently, 'We'll have to go look for him.'

'All right,' Ames said blandly. 'He's

47

probably tying on the nosebag—he sure couldn't afford to eat in this dump.'

They descended the stairs. Ignoring the curious stares of the clerk, Ames steered her into the deserted lounge. 'Why don't you wait here? No sense both of us buckin' that wind.'

Something left its quick track across the jab of her glance.

Ames said, lowering his voice, 'Don't be a fool! You either trust me or you don't, and if you don't we might as well call it quits now.'

She considered him uneasily, then sank into a chair.

Ames went into the bar. He bought three cigars, putting two of them away, pausing in the lobby to fire up the third. While hunting a place to get rid of the match, his glance crossed the clerk's. The man's bulging stare wheeled Ames toward a window.

Out in the wind-whipped dust two men, close together, faced each other in unmistakable anger. They stood before a saloon whose thrust-open batwings held a clot of silent watchers. Up and down the street other men were stopped, held by the imminence of violence.

The bigger of the pair was the granger Ames had clashed with.

There was a gun in the waistband of his baggy-kneed pants. He had one big-knuckled hand, like a cur on a leash, whitely wrapped about its grip. There was no doubt about his intention. Armed, and with enough rotgut in him to be insultingly reckless, he was plainly determined to hooraw the other into making some move that would give him an excuse.

A shift in the wind brought a snatch of his talk. 'You goddam cow wallopers think you're bigger'n Jesus H. Christ!' And, again: 'Guess you got a big laff runnin' your stock through my crops. Le's see how big you are now—fill your hand!'

The cowman was livid. He was shaking with fury when a broad-shouldered gent in a black flat-crowned hat shoved out of the crowd and, without even bothering to open his mouth, grabbed the pair of them by the scruff of their necks and resoundingly whacked their heads together.

It was one of the swiftest, boldest feats of dexterity and quick-thinking courage Ames had ever witnessed. When the fellow let go of them, both men went limber-legged into the dust. The man coolly bent, came up with their guns, and walked off. Then he was in the lobby, shutting the door against the driving wind.

'God A'mighty, Parson!' somebody exclaimed. 'You mighta got your head blowed off!'

The man, paying no attention, crossed to the desk and laid the pistols down. 'Better keep these, Farley, till Wheeler and Gentry get back a little savvy.'

The clerk hurriedly thrust the guns under the

49

counter, afterward rubbing his hands on his pants legs. Still appearing a mite green about the gills, he nodded nervously. 'That crazy farmer ain't like to quit till he gets himself killed.'

His glance, touching Tara, wheeled to find Ames. 'There you are! This is him—Preacher Pearce. Reverent,' he grinned, 'meet Hollister Ames. Him an' that girl there figures to get hitched.'

The preacher's eyes, passing Ames, gravely considered Tara's flushed cheeks. He was the man she had seen from the door of Ames' room, the one who'd said he hoped she'd be comfortable.

CHAPTER SEVEN

She found neither challenge nor reproach in the way he stood regarding her. A great tolerance appeared, as though all his life had brushed elbows with sin, and nothing Hell tried could surprise or dismay him.

Tara, embarrassed, was sure he must know she'd spent the night with Ames, shut up behind walls like a Scarlet Woman. She didn't want his forbearance, his understanding! Humiliated, frightened, writhing with guilt and confusion, she turned away her burning cheeks, fiercely resenting his continued silence.

What business was it of his what she did! *He* didn't have to stay out there, hardly more than a peon at Mike's beck and call! Pushed, shaken by the violence of her thoughts, Tara found herself alone with the man, boxed into a corner with no idea how she'd got there.

'Child,' he said, 'why are you shaking?'

'I'm *not* shaking—and I'm not a *child!*'

It came out too loud. Over there, where that bunch from the dining room were mumbling, the talk fell away in a twisting of heads. Tara, glaring defiantly, despised every one of them.

'We are all of us children,' the preacher said gently, 'in the sight of the Lord. We are all greatly tempted. It is sometimes hard to know what is right. Perhaps—'

Tara looked about wildly but couldn't find Ames. A terrible sense of aloneness engulfed her.

Pearce said: 'He'll be back. Are you quite sure, Miz Drood, you understand what you are doing?' The power of his eyes compelled her attention; they were gray, deep, probing. 'You should think about this. There's a lot more to marriage than the good times and laughter. There are a heap of tomorrows in a marriage. You'll not always agree with each other, you know. You'll be tied for the rest of your life to this man.'

Tara's jaws were clenched.

Pearce regarded her gravely. An attractive girl. Petulant now, seething with guilt and

51

resentment, frightened, rebellious; yet there was something appealing about her. She was commonplace enough—almost earthy, he decided uncomfortably. There was a pride about her, though. It was in the turn of her head, the thrust of her chin, her sparkling anger.

He sensed other things, too. Behind her selfishness, a willfulness that reminded him of Mike. She was awkwardly thin, too improbably frail to house so much turbulence, such a bursting aliveness that every contour, each change of expression, reflected it; the churning of a deep unrealized womanliness that unsettled and disturbed him almost as much as the look of those red lips. Unplumbed depths, a danger that drew him ... and softer things a man could work with and build on. The waste of these depressed him.

Ames was a cheap opportunist. With more experience she'd have seen this. It was something, however, no one else could explain to her, something she was going to have to find out herself. Considering what might happen should he flatly refuse to marry them, Pearce was forced to shake his head. She'd go off with Ames anyway.

Pearce got out his dog-eared Bible. If she could defy Mike Drood—and this was what it amounted to—nothing anyone else might say would matter.

Ames returned, urbane and smiling. Tara,

waiting stiffly by the desk, began to breathe more naturally. Pearce accepted the ribbon-tied paper the man reached across to him. It had gone beyond talk now, but when Ames fetched Tara away from the desk Pearce, when they stood in front of him, asked: 'You're certain, ma'am, this is what you want?'

A jostle of shapes from the archway edged closer. Ames turned livid. 'Would I be here, else?' Tara said with her chin up.

Ames, relaxing, chuckled maliciously.

Pearce said, 'Clasp hands,' and flipped open his Bible. 'Dear God,' he said, lifting up his eyes, 'we humbly beseech Thee, for all sorts and conditions of men, that thou wouldst be pleased to make Thy ways known to them, and let Thy saving grace guide and comfort these who have come to be joined today. God, from whom cometh down every perfect gift, we praise Thy Name for all thou hast vouchsafed us, for health and strength, for the abundance about us; and if there be any special mercies not present to our minds in this moment, we thank thee for them.'

Tara's mouth tightened.

'"Dearly beloved,"' Pearce intoned, and went into the ritual, the words carrying solemnly through the quiet room. Out on the street, a dog barked persistently.

'"Do you, Tara Drood, take this man for your husband, world without end, in sickness and in health, through hard times and plenty,

53

for better and for worse until death do you part?"'

Eyes defiant, Tara said, 'I do.'

'"And do you, Hollister Ames" ... that i. your name, isn't it?'

'Of course it's my name!'

'The Lord can hear. No need for shouting "And do you, Hollister Ames, take this woman for your wife through good times and bad, in sickness and health, world without end unti death do you part?"'

Ames, still scowling, said testily, 'I do!'

Pearce looked around. '"Does anyone know of any reason why these two should not be joined in holy wedlock?" If so, speak up.'

'What about Old Mike?' the nosy clerk said Tara's chin lifted. Ames glared when one of the crowd from the dining room sniggered.

Pearce said dryly, 'Put the ring on hei finger.'

Ames' hands were shaking, but he got the ring on her. 'Let us pray,' Pearce said, and dragged out the silence until every head was bent.

'O Lord Jesus Christ, who hast made me and redeemed me and brought me where I am upon my way, Thou knowest what Thou wouldst do with these Thy children; do according to Thy will, with mercy. Amen.'

When they looked up, Pearce said, '] pronounce you man and wife in the sight of God. It is customary, Mr Ames, for the groom to kiss the bride.'

The cattle buyer pecked Tara's cheek. The crowd grinned. No one offered to shake Ames' fist. Pearce went over to the desk with the license and wrote his name. He got the clerk and another man to sign as witnesses and gave the certificate to Mrs Ames. 'I hope you'll be mighty happy, ma'am.'

Ames tossed two four-bit pieces, three nickels, and a dime on the counter, grabbed his wife by the elbow and, without a word, hustled her off up the stairs. Most of the coins rolled onto the floor. Pearce, without even a backward glance, put on his hat and walked out of the place.

Upstairs, Ames caught up his belongings and flung them into a bag. He wheeled to where Tara stood, wide-eyed and silent. 'Come on— we're gettin' out of this dump.'

'But the doctor...' she said.

He picked up his bag, herded her out of the room.

The crowd was gone when they got to the lobby. 'Just a minute,' the clerk said as they were heading for the door. 'That'll be three dollars each.'

'Charge it to Star Circle,' Ames growled, and strode on. Tara was too upset to speak. She followed Ames out to the street. 'We'll have to get a rig,' he said.

'Shine, mister?'

Ames scowled at the boy. 'Where's the

55

nearest livery?'

'Tanner's. Two blocks down an' one to th
right. Sure you don't want me to shine—'

Ames strode off, Tara hurrying after him
'You mind if I catch my breath?' she said, ha
running to keep up. Ames waited impatientl
till she got hold of his arm.

She couldn't think what he was so rile
about. This wasn't at all the kind of thing sh
had dreamed of, but he was tired, of course
and upset, just as she was. It would work ou

Mrs Hollister Ames.

Here was the one thing they couldn't tak
away. Through all her confusions Tara hugge
it to her. Let Mike find someone else to slop hi
hogs—she was done with it. The thought of th
ranch did not seem quite so dismal now tha
she knew she didn't have to go back.

Of course, she would, but she didn't have t
stay. Let him yell! Never again would she hav
to give in to his old man's notions. Ames ha
changed all that.

Ames had freed her.

CHAPTER EIGHT

By the time they got to the stable Tara'
husband appeared to have got over whateve
had ailed him. He seemed more his natural sel
again, no longer withdrawn and preoccupied
56

he even flashed her a bit of a smile as he shortened his stride, accommodating it to her own skirts-hampered gait. 'We'd like a horse and buggy,' he told the whiskered codger who came limping up.

'I can see,' the stableman said, 'you're a gent that won't take nothin' but the best.' He grinned at Tara as he whipped off his hat. 'Buy or hire?'

'What's the odds?'

'We got a real fast-stepper I'd say would just about come up to your style. Trouble is, the boss-man says she's not to be rented. Steeldust. Fourteen three. Four-year-old blood bay. Purty a piece of hoss as you'll find in a week's solid ridin'.'

'Let's look,' Ames said skeptically. 'You say she's fast?' They followed the gimpy hostler around to a clutter of pens and sheds straggling over five acres of dust and weeds.

'An' gentle as a lamb. You could stake her to a hairpin,' Whiskers declared enthusiastically. 'There she is'—he waved, pulling up before a pole corral with a lean-to attached—'a real gentleman's horse, and sound as a dollar.'

Tara watched while Ames went over the mare. He stood back a bit, thinking. 'Mind if I go in?'

'If you kin fault her, the drinks are on me.'

Tara thought the horse was the flossiest mare she had ever clapped eyes on. The bay carried herself like a queen. Short-coupled on top, with a long underline, clean limbed, well muscled, with a chest that looked wide and deep as Geronimo's, and little pin ears flickering round to each sound like the horns on a snail, she was a beauty, all right.

Tara asked, 'What do you call her?'

Whiskers said with a snort, 'The names some people gives hosses is a sure-enough caution!' He watched Ames prodding and poking, watched him pick up her feet one after the other. 'Boss calls her Gitana—across the Line that means Gypsy.'

Ames came out of the pen. 'Will she drive?'

'Mister, that mare cut her teeth on a buggy shaft.'

'How much do you figure on holding me up for?'

'Tell you the truth, if she was mine you'd never get her. But the boss says she goes— nothin's sacred t' that feller.' He peered at Ames sleepily. 'How's three hundred sound to you?'

'Let's go,' Ames told Tara.

'Man,' Whiskers said, 'what you got in your veins?'

Ames herded Tara toward the street.

The hostler, scowling, limped after. 'Hold on,' he growled, 'you've caught me with m tradin' pants on. How's about two fifty?'

Ames neither slowed nor swerved.

'Two hundred!' Whiskers whimpered, like every tooth in his head was hurting. 'Man
58

that's *stealin'!*'

Ames thought so too. He kept right on going. Tara said, 'There's nothing wrong with—'

Ames didn't stop to do any arguing. As they came up to the stable, he said with his lip curled: 'I don't figure to give my back teeth away. For fifty dollars—'

The hostler snorted. 'That money won't even buy dogs in this town!' He stopped, and stood glaring. He spat disgustedly, caught up a manure fork and headed for a barrow in one of the distant runways.

Ames came around. 'Name your bottom price.'

Whiskers peered over his shoulder, then stopped. He leaned against his fork. 'I don't mind tellin' you this goes agin' the grain, but as it happens you're the first gent that's come in here this mornin'. Boss'll raise the rafters if I let you go outa here empty-handed.' He considered Ames slanchways. 'Give me one fifty an' we'll call'er sold.'

*   *   *

'Done,' Ames said, 'if that includes a buggy.'

'You're kiddin',' Whiskers grinned.

As Ames took hold of Tara's elbow, Whiskers snarled, 'I can't throw in no buggy at that price!' He watched Ames edge the girl through the door. He said, gritting his teeth,

59

'Will you take one on loan?'

Ames winked at Tara. 'We'll be waiting out front.'

Ten minutes later Whiskers joined them with the rig.

Ames walked around it and handed Tara up. He stowed his bag in back of the seat and climbed in himself. He picked up the lines. 'Which road do I take for the Twin Peaks country?'

'End o' this street'll take you right into it.' The man's eyes winnowed down as Ames reached for the whip. 'Ain't you fergittin' somethin'?'

'Bill of sale? Send it out to Star Circle. Old Mike'll take care of it. Giddap!' he cried, and put the whip to the mare.

*   *   *

The evening sun was wheeling low behind the banked haze of an overcast sky when they caught up with Doc at Bar 7 Ranch. They'd set off without food and found no place to get any. Both of them, cramped from the long, cold ride, were out of sorts when Ames pulled up in the unlovely clutter of what passed for buildings out here at the tail end of nowhere.

Bar 7, by the look of the straggly crops, was a nester layout and, like most of its kind, a depressing sight.

A soddy dug into the side of a hill served to

house the family, who answered to the name of LeGrue. The man, known as 'Bat,' was a reedy type with the unlikeliest ears Ames had ever encountered. They stood out from his bullet-gray head like wings. The only help he seemed to have was a yardful of tow-headed offspring ranging from Ticker, the oldest, who looked to be in his late teens and had a hacking cough, to Pukie, who was bald and still using her knees for transportation.

Maddie, the mother, again plainly carrying, told them the doc would be out pretty quick now. He was working over Pazzle, the youngest boy, aged three, who had mighty near chopped off four toes with the ax.

Tara said: 'This is Hollister Ames—I'm his wife. Holly's a cattle buyer for Crimp, Crane, and Cranston—the St Looey packin'-house people.'

Maddie said: 'It was plumb lucky for us the doc was over to the Mayhew place with a birthin'. Been there all night, I guess—what was left of it time he got there.' She peered at Tara. 'Ain't you the Drood girl? Sure favor him ... Yes, Clinchy rode after the doc soon's Pazzle done it. It's a-gittin' so's you just can't hardly leave nothin' around.'

The doctor, a mousy old man preceded by a scuffed and battered-looking grip whose handle at one end appeared to be attached by hardly anything more substantial than faith, came out of the soddy with a gusty sigh. His

61

eyes found Maddie. 'I'll look in on him again first chance I get. Keep him quiet and off that foot.'

Maddie sighed, too. 'I'll sure do the best I kin, Doc.' She pushed hair off her cheek. 'This here's the Drood girl, Old Mike's granddaughter. Feller with her's a St Looey packer. Somebody ailin' over to your place?' she asked across him.

Doc's glance touched Ames and came back to Tara: 'You've shot up some since the last time I saw you. How's your ma?'

'It's Mike,' Tara said.

'What's the matter with him?'

'We don't rightly know. He's been spoonin' that mule medicine into him again. Been flat on his back for pretty near a week.'

Doc nodded. 'Thinks he's a white-oak post—always did. Can't tell him anything.' He took a squint at the sky. 'I'll get over there quick's I can.' He looked back at Maddie. 'You keep that boy in bed for a week.'

'I'll git your horse,' Bat said, hitching his pants up.

'Nice meeting you,' Ames nodded, herding Tara toward the buggy.

Maddie cried, 'Land sakes! you ain't goin' yet, be you?' Bat, twisting around, called over his shoulder, 'You're sure as hell welcome t'stay fer grub, if you don't mind takin' it away from the little ones.'

They pulled into Stroud just short of three. The only lights showing were in the Buffalo Bull, a sporting house with bar attached. Ames peered at his wife, decided she was asleep, and wondered if he'd time to step into the place for a couple of quick ones. His mouth was dry, he'd run out of cigars, his stomach was shoved right up against his backbone and every joint ached as though it had been put through a wringer. Even the mare looked ready to quit, and he had grazed her twice since leaving Bar 7.

Ames stared at the Bull in a stupor of exhaustion. While he was still trying to separate his thoughts from his thirst, the mare pulled over to the Bull's rail, and stopped.

Tara hauled her chin off her chest and looked around, blinking in the lights. 'What are we doing here?'

'Ask the horse,' Ames grunted.

Tara rubbed her face. 'Hotel's back there across from the bank.'

'No lights,' Ames said.

'They keep a bell on the counter.'

Ames picked up the lines, too beat to argue.

But the mare wouldn't budge. Not even the whip or the swung weighted butt of it was able to persuade her to lift one hoof.

Ames got out and grabbed hold of the cheek strap. He tugged, swearing. He cajoled. He used highly inflammable language, to all of which Gitana turned a very deaf ear. Ames stared at her, furious.

'Oh, come on,' Tara said, getting down a bi stiffly. 'I'm too tired and cold to stand around any longer.'

Ames said viciously, 'I ought to beat he goddam brains out!' But Tara was already moving away. With a final ugly snarl, Ames stomped after her.

*   *   *

Neither one of them seemed to be in a mood to remind the other that this was their wedding night. 'No need of waking anyone up,' Tara said. She got a key off the rack. Ames followed her down the hall.

They got undressed in the dark without conversation. Tara got into the cold bed, doubling her legs up. Ames opened his bag and got out a nightshirt. He stood there a minute, then pitched it aside.

CHAPTER NINE

Tara, when they reached Star Circle in the blustery shank of the next afternoon, made a considerable stir among the retainers with the perfumed finery of her citified clothes. In the excitement scarcely anyone appeared to notice the elegant stranger whose gloved hands held the lines.

Ames, perspiring, was keenly aware of the hazardous nature of his presence.

The fortlike structures were fashioned of heavy adobe, shrewdly grouped and impregnably protected by a massive wall spanning the gut of the gorge which held them. Beneath this, through iron culverts, burst a roar of water, some year-around river tumbling down from the heights. The buildings were flanked by brindled slopes whose rock faces thrust sharply upward and disappeared into climbing timber.

Ames had come in over a bridge of loose planks that had clattered and rattled like castanets. Great gates swung inward to allow them entrance; now Ames got his first real look at the house, at the sheds and corrals backed against the valley's end.

A dog rushed out, fierce with its barking. Ames had his hands full with the mare. He saw men moving about the distant pens and wondered what had happened to the roundup. There was a nearer, excited flutter of petticoats and cotton pantalones where a huddle of house servants jabbered and stared. A man stood on the house porch, eyes scrinched unreadably, watching them drive up.

Someone called off the dog.

Ames brought the buggy around before the porch (a gallery, really) and pulled up alongside it, thinking this man, who was armed and wore spurs, hadn't the proper heft to be Drood. He had the eyes for it, though, and the voice. 'Fetch 'im right in,' he called, half turning to yell, 'Elfego!—see to the mare.' He whipped a look to the girl. 'What kep' you? Old Man's taken a turn for the worst.'

'You mean the doc hasn't got here?'

The man's regard gleamed with censure as he noted Tara's garb. This look, freighted with hostility, settled heavily on Ames. 'Git down,' he growled.

Ames got stiffly out of the buggy and stepped around to help Tara, but she was down before he reached her. Her eyes looked nervous. 'This is Jock,' she began, 'Jock Meyers, Mike's ramrod—'

'Better git right in there, Missy.' Crusty glance still on Ames, Meyers said, 'I'll see that this feller gits paid off an' fed.' He waved Elfego away with the mare.

'This "feller,"' Tara cried with flushed cheeks, 'is my *husband*,' and glared, furious.

Meyers rubbed the scrape of his stare into Ames. 'You better not let the Ol' Man ketch wind of it. He'll run this pimp hell west an' crooked.'

Ames turned livid but didn't open his mouth. Tara's eyes skewered around in a look of pure astonishment.

A contemptuous bark of a laugh came out of Meyers. He went striding off.

When Ames' brain started functioning again, the iron-stiff back of the Star Circle boss was disappearing toward the tangle of interlocked corrals. Ames told himself he would cut that bastard's heart out; but the damage was already done, and he knew it.

*   *   *

In her grandfather's room Tara stood beside the old man on the bed. The winkless immobility of his stare was indescribably unnerving. He was not like himself at all, so still, so strangely shrunken. He didn't seem big, lying there in his sun-faded shirt and patched jeans with his scuffed boots dustily tangled in the spread. He looked pitifully frail and defenseless.

It made her say defiantly, 'I'm married now—do you hear? I said I'm *married!*'

She half expected him to spring from the bed.

He did not move. The waxlike face showed nothing; she might have thought him dead except for the uneven rasp of his breathing.

She couldn't understand this quiet acceptance. She felt a touch of shame and cried at him fiercely: 'I'm through being your peon—you hear? I've got a husband now! I'll do as I please!'

She felt a fool to be standing there, glaring at a man who refused to open his mouth. 'Why

don't you yell?' she demanded rebelliously
'Why don't you threaten to cut me off?'

She might as well have shouted at a rock. She
was left without weapons against the shame
that rushed over her. She guessed she was still
upset about Ames letting Meyers make him
look like a whip-threatened cur.

She could see Ames' side of it—a stranger
here, newly kin, but Meyers' remarks still
rankled. There were some things a man
couldn't ignore around here ... not and keep
folks' respect. Respect was something that, to
Tara, had suddenly become extraordinarily
important.

She glared at Mike. It was almost as though
he had got the best of her. She had come here
braced for an explosion and all he did was
stare! She must be loco, imagining she read pity
in that look.

Unable to stomach such a notion, she quit
the room and went in search of her mother,
finding her, as she expected, silently sitting in
the dirt-floored kitchen like a dozing *bruja*
[witch].

*   *   *

It was hard to realize Jesusita had been a
handsome woman. There was little to suggest it
in that gray-brown wrinkled face, in the
gnarled old hands and pipestem arms that
hugged her withered body. She complained of

68

the cold, was seldom seen without the poor shawl draped over her bent shoulders, the high-backed comb in its froth of black lace ludicrous above the stringy pulled-tight hair.

She was apparently as deaf as an oxcart to everything not pointedly brought to her attention. And when she spoke it was mostly in grunts—not that she hadn't linguistic ability. She could display, when it suited her, a blunt turn of speech that could leave a man's hide dangling about him in strips. Most frequently she used the tongue of her fathers, perversely indifferent to its effect on those spoken to. She took an unreasonable pride in being crossgrained and obstinate.

'Do you have to sit there?' Tara cried when her mother continued to ignore her. More and more Jesusita, as the days slipped by, appeared to be retiring into the habits of a squaw. Tara said, exasperated, 'Have you no curiosity about what kept me?'

Her mother said in Spanish, 'A man, of course—what else? Did he buy those clothes in addition to your virtue?'

Tara thinly smiled. 'I am married. I'll be leaving this place ... *Do you hear?*' she asked sharply.

'I hear. Your father said that, too.' One lifted hand made the Sign across her breast. 'He had very fine dreams. I would look like Carlotta ... we were going to Durango; he had the offer of a partnership. A-a-ai-hé!'

She scowled at the fire, sighed again and got up. 'Nobody leaves this place. It is a millstone hung about your grandfather's neck.'

She slap-slapped over to the smoke-streaked maw of the hand-patted Indian-style beehive fireplace, peered into a simmering pot, and came back. 'Nobody leaves this place,' she said brightly.

'*I* will leave.'

'May the devil be deaf.'

Tara's lip curled. 'I am not his peon! I will leave when I want.'

The old woman seemed lost in the fog of her memories. Poor Mamacita, Tara thought. So terribly old, so bent and wizened. She was like a child with her crazy talk.

In the flickering firelight the anguished Christ hung like ivory on His cross.

Tara was turning to leave when Jesusita said, 'This man you have bought with your body—where is he?'

'On the porch.' Tara's face came around. 'Did you think he was waiting at More Oaks? We're married, I tell you! We came in a buggy!' She said, unable to hold in her anger, 'We will take the big room—'

Her mother, brushing past, went slapping off down the hall. She was back almost at once. 'A foreigner, a robber not even of the country!' She snorted her contempt.

Tara choked back her anger. 'We will have the canopied bed.'

70

'Your grandfather—'

'I have some rights!'

'You think so?' Little birds looked out of her mother's eyes. 'Have you increased this place by so much as one codo? Did you drive off los Indios? hang the picaros? ripen the grapes in their season? God deliver us, I thought not!'

The old woman's hands drew the shawl closer round her. 'By what then have you rights? By living here?' Malice sharpened her features. 'Do I not live here myself—and half a hundred vaqueros? Ho! Even the fingers on one's hand are not equals. Who would eat the calf must swing the rope. And where is the médico you went to that town for?'

'We followed him all the way to Twin Peaks—he said he would come, but he is only one man. Other people have sickness—'

'Other people! And without the Old One, where would these be?'

'Times change. Even when I was going to the school it was different,' Tara said defensively. 'In More Oaks they do not care for Mike. He is not called patrón around there, but a range hog. He stands in the way—'

'Enough!' The old woman snorted. 'In that town they are fools, and you a bigger one for listening.' She looked her scorn. 'I can at least see the length of my nose.'

'And what do you see?'

'I see blood, and more blood—I cannot see the end of it. But this I know: of what he claims,

71

not a blade of grass will be turned while he lives—'

'Does he own the world?'

'What he owns he will keep.'

'And when he's gone?' Tara said.

'Then the coyotes will come.'

'This place will be mine—'

'It will fall apart. No woman can hold it.'

'You're forgetting.' Tara smiled. 'I have a husband.'

The old woman sniffed. 'Expect nothing of a cat except its skin.'

CHAPTER TEN

Hoofs and wheels came out of the night, their arrival announced by the bridge's hollow thunder. The dog charged growling as the gates skreaked open, the ramrod's voice curtly slicing the racket. Tara ran through the house and out onto the gallery to stand beside Ames in the darkness.

'Who is it?' she called.

'Sounds like Doc,' Ames muttered.

Meyers called away the dog and two men, vaguely seen, got out of the rig, the one with the bag coming on toward the house. A mozo's cotton pantalones appeared in the yellow blob of a lantern which Meyers took and held up.

The ramrod said, 'What do you want here

Harry?'

In the nimbus of the lantern, the rawboned man Meyers was facing threw a considerable shadow. You could not make out his look but Ames felt Tara stiffen.

Meyers said, 'It'll have to wait—he's flat on his back.'

'Harry Chalkchild,' Tara whispered as the doctor came onto the porch with his bag. She took him off into the house to see Mike.

There was no observable change. The doctor passed a hand several times before his face, pulled back a lid and took hold of Mike's wrist. 'How do you feel?'

Tara thought it was evident the old man wasn't about to move any mountains. Doc fussed around, softly clucking. He got out a bottle of pills and a syringe, into which he fixed a needle. He looked at Tara over his shoulder. 'You can run along now.'

'What's the matter with him?'

'We'll get to that.'

'Won't you need help?'

The doctor said irascibly, 'When I do I'll ask for it.'

Choking back her anger, Tara went into Mike's office.

Chief amongst her irritations was her husband's meek acceptance of Meyers' remarks and manner. Jesusita's contempt was even more disquieting. They were both set against him but this, Tara reminded herself,

73

was natural because he was an outlander and, worse still, a *Yankee*.

Of course they resented a stranger coming in. Meyers had been top screw for as long as Tara could remember. He had the Old Man's notions ground deep into him. Meyers was nothing but an extension of Mike. Bigoted, brash, as unquestioningly Star Circle as that damned dog or the army of Mexicans that lived on the place.

Yet she had to believe it would all work out. They didn't know Ames yet, that was all.

Her thoughts went to Chalkchild. Why was he here? She found it hard to regard Apaches as anything more human than a pack of snarling wolves. The government was crazy, pampering such savages. Give them half a chance, Mike said, and they'd claw your goddam guts out.

Those grangers, too, backing up around More Oaks, lay heavy on her mind. The whole range was becoming concerned over the way those fools were piling into this country, lured by ridiculous promises and claptrap. Every one of those nesters had his knife out for Mike. Star Circle's gun-hung riders were holding them away from too much grass they'd been told they could have for the taking.

Her mother had been right. There'd be blood spilled before this range saw the last o them. The weather would whip them; only by the time the weather got around to it, thi country wouldn't be fit for a snake. There wa bound to be trouble. A cowman's life was full of it.

It was no skin off her nose. She wasn't going to be here.

Going out to the gallery, she slid into a chair she pulled up beside Ames.

'How is he?' Ames asked.

Tara shrugged. 'He'll get over it.' She was trying to think how to handle this. A man's pride had to be considered.

'When he's up and about,' she said finally, 'you're going to have to take a firm hand with him.'

'In what way?'

'Well ... you got off on the wrong foot. The only thing Meyers understands is facts. Same with Mike.'

'It didn't seem hardly the place for a scene.' He said presently, through the thin smoke of his cigar, 'Who's this feller that came out with the doc?'

'We'll get to him later. What you've got to get straightened out pronto is your place in this deal as my husband. You're going to have to insist on bein' noticed and thought about. Particular with Mike—we can't send *him* packin'.'

'We'll get along,' Ames said stiffly.

'You let Mike do the gettin' along.'

Ames said gruffly, 'A man can use a little tact—'

'What's that?'

75

He screwed around some, got his butt canted more to the fit of the chair. 'If one of them should say to me, "Clean out the stables," I wouldn't give him any lip. I just wouldn't do it.'

She stared a long while at the blob of Ames' face.

'After all,' he said, bridling, 'we're—'

'You ain't hard of hearin', are you?'

'All a man has—'

'Don't you understand my lingo?'

'There are certain amenities, adopted rules of conduct, a person has to observe. Civilized people don't—'

'The only rule around here is what suits Mike. Better get it through your head. The next thing,' Tara said, 'is to change it, and you ain't goin' to change anything by gettin' out your handkerchief.'

'Good Lord! Are you suggesting every time something rubs me wrong, I'm to reach for a pistol?'

'You want to wind up like my father?'

Ames said, 'We don't have to be all that drastic, do we?'

'I'd hate to think I been mistaken in you.'

Ames looked to where the cook, in the lamplit door of his shack, stood banging on a washtub. 'Come an' git it, you rannies, 'fore I th'ow it away!'

'I've no intention,' he said, 'of knuckling under to anyone, but I'm not going at this like a bull in a chicken yard. You can't just grab all your problems by the horns—be reasonable, Tara. I don't like this any better than you do, but people have to be practical. Change takes a lot of getting used to. You got to give it plenty of room.'

He watched the shapes crowding into the cookshack.

'Sometimes,' Tara said, getting onto her feet, 'you *have* to grab the horns. Ever seen anybody laugh a gun barrel out of his way? That's what you'll be up against if you don't get in some mighty quick licks.'

Ames got up and patted her shoulder. 'Just give me a couple of—'

'Come on, let's eat.' She pulled open the door.

'But damn it, Tara—'

'You heard what Meyers said. Face them down or they'll have you running hell west an' crooked.'

*   *   *

Mike was gone when they got up the next morning. Slipped away in the night, Jesusita told them, devoutly crossing herself. The doc said his heart had just plain wore out.

Tara could feel Ames covertly attempting to catch her eye, but she went on with her eating, letting him squirm. In town he could deal with pretty near anything. But when it came to what lay ahead of them, Tara guessed she was going to have to pull on the pants.

There'd be a thousand things to see to. She simply dared not risk her husband's involvement in anything so closely affecting her future. She knew these people. They might resent being forced to deal with a woman but it was her option, not theirs.

Maybe Old Mike had got the last laugh, leaving her saddled with this place. But she didn't have to *keep* the dammed spread—she didn't even *have* to sell it. She had no one to suit any longer but herself.

It was a breath-clutching thing to become suddenly aware that on a hundred thousand acres the only law was what you wanted. She was a little dizzy with the magnitude of her own changed status.

CHAPTER ELEVEN

Three hundred thousand acres of grass!

It made a good round sound rolling over Tara's tongue, as it did more than once during the next several hours, obscuring the harsh memories, the hatefulness that always before had been so integral a part of every thought about this place. Someway the ranch did not seem to weigh so insufferably upon her now that the rock of Mike's termagant displeasure no longer hung over the choices she migh

78

make.

She was finally free, free to go her own way ... yet there was an undeniable excitement inherent in knowing there was nothing to prevent her stepping into the Old Man's boots. She was, in fact, Star Circle now.

Riders came and went. One fellow she dispatched to the roundabout outfits to pass along the day and hour of the proposed last rites. Another was sent to notify the law and fetch the undertaker; it was his job, too, to request the early presence of her grandfather's lawyer, the banker and the hell-chaser, Pearce.

She felt an inexplicable reluctance about including the preacher. Visions of him nagged her like an ulcerated tooth. While she stubbornly refused to inquire into this, she understood well enough that she was going to have to have him. Folks would expect it. They'd come from miles around, needing to see with their own eyes that the human avalanche which for an eternity had been so dreadfully crouched above them was, indeed, to be feared no longer.

Yet these very persons—drawing, perhaps, the first free breaths they'd enjoyed in years— would be the loudest to protest if the expected words were not reverently spoken over the remains. In effect it would be like burying Caesar. You couldn't put away a country's Number One Citizen like you would a dead mule. She had to have a sky pilot. And Benton

Pearce, who had walked straight into a gunfight and stopped it, was the only one available.

She gave a deal of thought to Ames as well, casting around in her mind what to do with him. As her husband he would have to be kept in the foreground; his charm and handsome presence must be made to count for all they could. But, after last night, she was worried about trusting him ... with a talking part, anyway. Tempers being what they were around here, early impressions could...

Tara's thoughts jumped around like a boxful of crickets. She was still strongly minded to get away from Star Circle, but giving over its control was something else again. Unexpected, almost *dizzying*, sensations went palpitating through her whenever she remembered that she and this ranch were now practically synonymous. No yackety bunch of damned coyotes was going to take it away from her!

She was like a small dog with a very large bone. Hanging onto this place began to look like being her duty, something owed to Old Mike.

Calling Ames into the office, she sent for Jock Meyers. She said, while they were waiting: 'Just look smart. I'll do the talking.'

'Do you imagine,' Ames said skeptically, 'he's going to take orders from a woman?'

She sat down at Mike's desk, looking very determined. Her stare settled uncomfortably on Ames. 'Don't bust in without I ask for your opinion. Never mind what you think. If I ask, back me up.'

It was clear Ames did not relish the role of indulgent husband. Finally, scowling, he grumbled, 'All right.'

The range boss came in, his look flashing over them. 'Well?' he said. He had the habit of command. An arrogant intolerance. Lip curled, standing there, he looked hard as a rock. It was this bleakness, the stare, that called up men's doubts and put the shakes in their legs. It was the man himself, the things the man stood for ... the power of Star Circle— and this was what Tara fastened on.

'You've been here quite a while,' she said.

'I was with the Old Man when he settled this place.'

'Satisfied?'

'Speak what's in your mind, Missy.'

'I've been thinking about replacing you.'

It was a startling thing, the way Jock Meyers threw back his head and laughed. With a sardonic twist of the mouth he wheeled away.

Tara cried angrily, 'I'm not through yet!'

He came around and, still grinning, scraped his stare across Ames.

'What,' Tara asked, 'did Chalkchild want?'

Meyers said, 'I'm handlin' that.'

'I'll decide,' Tara said, 'what's good for Star Circle.'

They glared at each other through

congealing silence. Ames, watching the range boss, experienced a sort of morbid dread. The man was so deep-seated in his case-hardened confidence, so brutalized by violence and by having his way, Ames half looked for him to strike the girl. Indeed, he did rock forward. The ruddy color rushed out of his cheeks, and in their gray furrows was an expression so horrid, so fiercely unreasoning, the self-declared cattle buyer almost cried out.

Tara's ungiving tones made Ames' knees knock together. She said: 'What did Harry want?'

'Same thing he's allus whinin' about—that lease money.'

'Lease . . . What lease money?'

'You didn't know about that?' Meyers showed a hard grin. 'About a third of this place is on Reservation lands, grass Mike's been leasin' from them goddam Apaches. Chalkchild argues they ain't been paid—'

'Have they?'

'Not lately,' Meyers admitted. 'Those rains, all this grass—there's no end to good beef! This lease was set up fer cash. Old Man hasn't got any, and no way to latch onto none without we unload a reg'lar hell's smear of cows. I've sold hides fer more'n you can git fer a cow today—'

'My husband,' Tara said, 'will take care of that. What did you tell Chalkchild?'

'Told him Mike was too busy to see him. But

he'll be back in a hurry when he finds out the Old Man has turned up his toes.'

'I'll talk with Harry—'

Meyers' scorn was apparent. 'Injuns won't do business with women.'

Tara's look never changed. 'What have you done with that beef?'

'Turned it back into the hills.'

'Well,' Tara said, 'you can trot it out again.'

Meyers reared back, staring at her incredulously. He drew a harsh breath. 'I guess not.'

'You knew those Indians would have to be paid.'

'They ain't been paid in two years! Where'll you get that kinda money? Old Man had no intention of payin'—'

'I'm running Star Circle. How long you continue to hold your job will depend,' Tara said, 'on how well you carry out my orders.'

Meyers swelled up like a toad. But clenched fists and ugly looks had no visible effect on Tara. She said coolly, 'I hope I've made myself clear.'

Meyers looked like something hacked out of rock as he stood with wild eyes trying to beat down her stare. Tara's glance never wavered. 'We'll want about thirty carloads—'

'Thirty cars won't be a patch to what we'll hev to dig out of them breaks if you're figurin' to pay off that lease in meat.'

'They'll be a start. I'm going to have Ames

83

give them a draft on Crimp, Crane and Cranston.'

'Injuns won't take paper.'

'Then we'll get cash from the bank. They'l take my husband's—'

Ames cried in a jumpity high-keyed voice 'They'll take cattle if that's all they can get... He backed away from Tara's look, frantic behind the shine of perspiration that broke across his cheeks. 'I mean...' He floundered swallowing nervously, eyes walling like those of a suddenly spooked bronc. He began to shake and Tara, twisting around, the better to examine him, said: 'Don't you feel well Hollister? Perhaps if you go lie down for a spell?'

'I'm all right. I just can't see wasting hard-to get cash when those filthy beggars would just as well settle...'

'It's a thought,' Meyers said, regarding Ames with more interest. 'We could drive some of that runty stuff in off the desert.'

'Whatever you think,' Tara nodded, 'just so they're satisfied.' She settled back in her chair. 'Be sure they're paid up to date and you get Harry's name on a paper to prove it.'

'There's a lot of unrest around More Oaks,' Ames put in. 'Place is crowded with settlers. If they can bring enough pressure, the government's liable to move out the Indians and throw those lands open.'

'If that should happen,' Tara said, 'we'd be

84

in much better shape on that grass with the lease paid. We'd be in better shape still if we were paid well ahead. I think you'd be smart to get a drive started pronto. Five or six of the boys should be able to handle it. Put the rest of the crew to rounding up beef. With what Hollister gets for those first thirty carloads—'

'I'd go easy there,' Ames urged, breaking in again. 'Next year the price might be considerably improved.'

'It couldn't hardly git worse.' The range boss nodded. 'I vote we should wait an' see what shapes up.'

Tara frowned. 'There's trouble shaping up—any fool can see that! How much of this range does Mike actually own? How much of it's patented?'

'About six hundred an' forty,' Meyers said. 'We've got the water sewed up—'

'We've got nesters on our grass, too. Why didn't Mike chase them out?'

'They come in since Mike's been down. I spoke to him about 'em,' Meyers grumbled, 'but he said leave 'em alone.'

'That don't sound like Mike,' Tara said.

Ames put in his oar again, suggesting that in view of the current unrest perhaps the old man had been too canny to stir up trouble. 'There's a lot of politicking going on. The railroad wants this country settled up. If the government moves the Indians, they'll throw open those Reservation lands—'

85

'If they do that,' Tara said, 'they'll throw open the rest of it, all the range we've got ou cattle on. We'd better start buying...' She sai with decision, 'Soon as Mike's buried, you ge a roundup started.'

Meyers shook his head. 'You can't hold lan without you show use of it.'

'You can hold it,' Tara said, 'if it's pai for—'

'We'd have to strip Star Circle to pay fer a that.'

'Then we'll strip it,' Tara said. 'You put th crew right on it.'

CHAPTER TWELVE

Ames hardly knew what to think now, but i was all too plain this deal was getting out o hand. Mike had conveniently croaked, but i no other way were things going as he' imagined.

Alarmed, he tried to pull himself togethe You wouldn't think an operation of thi magnitude could be so close to collapse. H bitterly cursed Mike for not in some wa nailing down the far-flung empire he ha cobbled together from force and threats; h could at least have run off those pukin nesters, not left them like a blazed trail for th hundreds of others pouring into More Oaks.

But the meanest surprise of all was the girl—Ames' child bride, whom he'd supposed would jump to his every whim. Overnight she'd become unpredictable. 'I thought,' he complained with a petulant frown, 'you was busting to get away from this place!'

'I was,' Tara nodded, coming out of her thinking. 'But we can't just go off and let the ranch fall apart. I had no idea things were in such bad shape. Perhaps'—she smiled with quick hope—'it's not as bad as it looks. Meyers naturally resents me. There's likely cash in the bank he doesn't know about. Mike was just bullying those Indians; that's the way he was. We can't go off now,' she said, glance darkening. 'That bunch at More Oaks are just waitin' for the chance to move in.'

She took a deep breath. Ames half wished, by God, he had never run across her. 'Mike was right'—she frowned—'about one thing: you've got to stand up for yourself in this world. You can't afford softness. Mike was right about that, too.'

Ames strode about the room.

'Why'd you butt in?' the girl demanded, remembering. 'I told you to let me do the talking—'

'You set him against us. That feller is goin' to make trouble,' Ames growled, but Tara brushed this aside.

'I'll take care of Jock. All you have to worry about is producing that draft once we get the

87

beef into those stock cars.'

'I thought we were going to pay off in cows...'

She brushed that aside, too. 'The Indians don't worry me.' She chewed at her lip. 'I'd sure like to know how much beef we've got to work with.' Her hazel eyes dug into him. 'You've *got* a draft, haven't you, for those first thirty carloads?'

The man was a picture of affronted dignity. 'You think a firm like Crimp, Crane and Cranston would send a buyer into the field empty-handed?' He got just the right amount of disgust into the tone, then something wheeled him sharply around to peer suspiciously.

'Light down,' she said on the edge of a smile. 'I just figured to be sure I wasn't countin' on something you couldn't produce.' She leaned back and stretched and got out of Mike's chair. She grinned at him then, almost without reservation. 'Think of it ... three hundred thousand acres of grass!'

Ames' lip curled sourly. 'With things like they are,' he said, watching her, 'we'd be smarter to sell and get out from under it.'

'You can't think what it means to me, what it does for me, Holly. I did want to get away— this place was like a...' She shook her head at him. 'With Mike gone, things are different. I see the possibilities. Anyway, nobody's got that kind of money. We'd take a whopping

88

loss—'

'We'll take a loss if you can't deal with those Injuns.'

'It isn't Chalkchild that bothers me. It's that bunch at More Oaks. That stupid Agent, that mob of plow chasers the railroad's been fetching in.' She looked at Ames darkly. 'Do you reckon the government will ever throw that land open?'

Ames said, 'It's happened. If you want to play safe, bust it up, sell it off to those peckerneck grangers for whatever you can get—before they take it away from you.'

He saw by her look, bitterly cursing himself, he had put her back up again, confronting her with a challenge. 'No one,' she said loftily, 'will take this place away from me!'

And she went off through the house, proud and ridiculous as a goddam Injun.

*   *   *

Left to his own devices Ames stood glaring across the sunlit yard. There was more to this girl than he'd figured. She might be led; she could never be driven. With her spindling shanks and child's expressions, the girl had made a fool of him.

It was infuriating to discover how sly she had been. Right from the time he'd named himself buyer for Crimp, Crane and Cranston, she had laid out to put a halter on him. It wasn't him

89

she'd wanted, but his packing-hou:
connections.

He fumed at the thought of how he'd bee
sucked into this mess. All the while he'd bee
figuring to better his prospects, she'd bee
leading him on, playing him like a damned c:
would a mouse! Even up in that room with tl
dress half tore off! Marriage had been in h
head every minute!

She had wanted a man between herself an
Mike. All Ames had been—or ever was like t
be, was a sonofabitching convenience!

God, how it graveled him! Biter bit, and by
chit of a girl! She must have known all alor
how bad in debt this place was. She wasn
blind to the danger of that bunch at More Oal
but was minded, in spite of them, to hold ont
everything.

Nobody not completely an idiot would try t
find logic in the actions of a woman. Maybe sl
had wanted to get away at first, but too muc
of Old Mike's bullheadedness was in her, th:
crazy pride of possession.

She had fallen in love with herself as mistre:
of the biggest ranch in the country. Sl
couldn't see that it was doomed, bound to t
riddled by that bunch of churn-twisters pilir
into More Oaks. She could no more hold ther
at bay than a crossfence could hold back a
avalanche. She was, in her own mind,
shrewder, younger edition of Mike. That tim
had changed meant nothing at all to her.

Faced with the inevitable end of all this, Ames, accustomed to hunting a quick profit, looked around for one. There were only two things on Star Circle a man could work with, grass and cows; and cattle, right now, weren't worth the trouble of stealing.

He took a look at the grass. He wasn't sticking around for any power of attorney. Wasn't minded to be here but long enough to see if there was anything left in that bank he could grab.

*   *   *

The sheriff and the long-faced undertaker from Stroud showed up in a rig while Ames and the girl, in the cavernous kitchen, were stowing away a bowl of frijoles. Jesusita, shriveled and wrinkled, sat over against the fireplace, lively as a mummy. Ames felt obliged to keep up the talk, but without any help it was falling a little flat when a mozo came in with news of the law. Ames shoved back from the table.

Tara said, 'They can wait in the yard.'

The servant went out. Ames said, scowling, 'Where's the sense in putting their backs up?'

He started to get out of his chair. Tara told him: 'That was Mike's style.'

Ames thought of how it had been last night in the middle of that enormous bed. He found it hard to believe, seeing her now so aggravatingly certain. He watched her mop out the bowl with a piece of folded tortilla. She got a Bull Durham sack off the mantel and put together a smoke, grinning at him over it as she ran the paper across her tongue. 'The sky won't fall.'

'Don't you Droods ever use any tact?'

Tara's lips thinned. The old woman loosed a quick gobble of words. Tara laughed. She looked back at Ames with the brightness of silver. She said, darkly smiling, 'Tact's what folks use when a gun barrel's pointed at their bellies.'

A cold shiver shook Ames, and he got nervously up and stumbled out of the room. He found himself staring at the canopied bed, the candlesticks, the hand-rolled mirror framed in Mexican tin.

She meant every goddam word of it!

CHAPTER THIRTEEN

Tara talked with the sheriff on the sunny front gallery while a mozo toured the undertaker off to see Mike. The sheriff's angular body, cramped into a rocker, appeared about as cheerless as his leathery cheeks. Too many years of tramping over the same ground with all his best thoughts cobblered by others had not notably readied him for charting a course through the shoals glimpsed ahead.

'Hard times,' he sighed. 'Whole country teemin' with beef, an' no market. When I was a kid you could sell hoofs 'n horns fer more'n you can git right now for the critter.' He fiddled with the brim of the hat in his lap. 'You keep your chin up. Jace'll find you a buyer if anyone can.'

'If you're talking about Jace Lathram, the banker...'

'He'll be out later on. Was tied up this mornin'.'

'He was never tied up when Mike wanted to see him.'

The sheriff peered reproachfully, and dug at an ear. 'Your grandpaw,' he sighed, 'was a pretty determined man. We are sure goin' to miss him.'

'I expect,' Tara said, 'you'll manage to bear up.'

The undertaker reappeared, looking properly subdued, and laid a hand on Tara's shoulder. He spoke as though each word were bathed in tears of personal loss. 'I'll be taking care of—'

'Then you'd better get a wiggle on. We're putting him away tomorrow. On that hill up there back of the corrals.'

The man looked startled. He half opened his mouth, but something in Tara's expression changed his mind.

Hoofs cut through the uncomfortable silence. The rocker skreaked as the sheriff

93

twisted around.

The new arrival stepped off his horse by th
bunkhouse. He was so gangling Tara almos
had to look twice to pick him out from th
fenceposts; then he turned. She saw the red hai
and the patches of freckles, the stubble tha
darkened the cut of gaunt cheeks. Sensin
something familiar, she watched him mov
into the grubshack.

The undertaker said, 'Ain't that Fludd? Th
one Joe Wheeler—'

'That's him,' the sheriff said. 'A ba
business.' He hitched up his mouth, swun
rheumy eyes back to Tara. 'Why don't you g
into town and put up at the hotel while you'r
waitin' for Jace to round up a buyer?'

Tara's smile looked brittle. 'I've no intentio
of selling.'

'No int—' He appeared incredulous. 'But
ma'am, you surely ain't figurin' to take hold o
this place? An outfit this size ... all thes
men...'

'I was brought up on this ranch. I've—'

'But a *woman*!' He looked aghast. 'Grea
Scott, ma'am!'

'What's wrong with that?' the gir
demanded. 'I'd like to know why men foreve
take it for granted all a woman can do is pu
grub on a table and flop on her back!'

The undertaker, his horrified stare rolled u
into his head, gave a kind of choked gasp an
beat a hasty retreat. The sheriff's cheek

turned white and then red as a love apple. He looked powerfully uncomfortable.

Before he could get back enough breath to splutter, Ames stepped out of the house and Tara said, 'My husband, Mr Hollister Ames of Crimp, Crane and Cranston.'

The lawman's eyes continued to goggle. Tara said, 'Sheriff Tolliver,' and Ames, smiling, extended a hand.

Tolliver pried himself out of the chair and briefly pumped it. 'Pleased t' meetcha.' He put his hat on. 'Reckon we better be gittin' back,' he said, and with another covert look slanched at Ames, moved into the yard and climbed aboard the buggy. The undertaker clucked.

Tara watched them drive off. 'So that's the local Hawkshaw.' Ames laughed. He got out a cigar, glancing whimsically at Tara. 'If that More Oaks bunch decide to farm this place, better let 'em have it. You'll get no help from him.'

Tara went into the house.

Ames shrugged, scratched a match, and puffed his cigar.

Just the business of that lease would have been bad enough. There was also Jock Meyers. All a man could get out of this place was trouble.

He consulted his watch. He had heard what Tolliver said about the banker. All the signs and signal smokes indicated the cupboard was going to prove bare. If there'd been any cash

95

balance to speak of, that banker would have built up a dust getting out here.

So you could write the bank off.

They'd know before the day got much older Drood hadn't been smart; he'd been almighty lucky. A pusher, and tough enough to make it stick with a bunch of scared fools who hadn't been any brighter than he was. If he'd been smart he'd have patented this spread, not depended on force to hold it together. A tough crew was no good once the government stepped in.

There was nothing insular in Ames' grasp of current politics. This business was happening all over the West; the government wanted the country settled. Railroads were bringing in farmers everywhere, and farmers were bellering for land and getting it. The Indians were in the same boat with the ranchers, with the buffalo before them. It was change, conform, or go under.

He glanced at the saddled mount ground-tied before the bunkhouse. He strolled over to the pens and stood looking at the horses. All colors and sizes. No better and no worse than you found most places, forty-dollar stuff bred from whatever was handiest. Ames knew horses; he had spent enough on them by and large to be an expert—and could still be taken in, as witness that mare he had bought in More Oaks.

He heard the crew come out of the

grubshack, the mumble of voices as they went off to get at the chores Meyers had handed out. Ames watched a couple of them taking off wheels and greasing hubs. He saw a wrangler go skallyhootin after the remuda. There'd be horses to shoe and tackle to straighten, the thousand and one tasks of starting a roundup. The men looked surly; they weren't looking forward to doing over a job just finished.

The girl was a fool. Never in this world could she rake up the amount it would take to nail down these sections. If the government decided to move out the Indians, it would be another Cherokee Strip, by God, the way them grangers would pile onto this land. Sure, you might kill a few. That wasn't going to stop them.

He got a rope off a saddle, went into the day pen, and caught up a horse, a big bald-faced dun. There was no use waiting around for that banker. Time to get out was right now while things were fluid.

He led the horse out and tied it, put the bars back in place. He got a bridle on his mount and slipped the bit between its teeth and was reaching for the saddle when someone came up and stopped at his shoulder. 'Where do you think you're off to?' Meyers said.

Ames lifted down the forty pounds of leather. 'You speaking to me?'

'Put it back,' Meyers said.

Ames chose to ignore him. The saddle went

slamming out of his hands. Ames came around in a fury of temper. 'Who the hell—'

He went back a step, the hard contempt in Meyers' stare turning him confused and uncertain. His cheeks began to burn, and he stood with clenched fists with his mouth still open and nothing coming out of it. Meyers' grin cut like a whip. Outraged, Ames cried, 'Who you think you're shoving around?'

'Nothin' that'll be missed if I should drop my foot on it. Now put that hull back where you found it.'

Ames' mouth turned dry. He was suddenly filled with a murderous frustration. He picked the saddle up. A shadow fell across his feet. He had a wild, nearly uncontrollable impulse to pitch the armful of leather straight into Meyers' face. But fear was stronger. Flopping the saddle across a pole, he slanched a venomous look at the man who'd come up and now was standing beside them.

Somewhere Ames had seen this face before, gaunt, beard-stubbled, and thatched with rust freckles.

'Don't let me catch you foolin' round here again.' Meyers, with a hard look, stepped aside. 'Now you scoot along back to the house with the women.'

*   *   *

Every writhing nerve in Ames' sweat-drenched

body made its own contribution to the turmoil inside him as he strode back and forth beside the canopied bed in a welter of emotions which threatened in their violence to shake him loose of any chance for calm analysis.

Burning with frustration, maddened by his impotence, he continued to go over again and again the craven exhibition he had made of himself. Meyers would never have dared lay a hand on him! He had stood there like some country lout and let that bastard make a fool of him!

Realizing this, and knowing his humiliation had been witnessed, only served the more to confound him. He couldn't scrape his thoughts together in the face of what that damned girl would think. The story would be all over ... Tara's big-city husband backing away from a hired hand! He could imagine the gusto such a tale would stir—he'd be laughed right out of the country.

Unless he did something.

He cursed in self-pity and confusion. The whole length of him shook with desires whose very wildness bruised him. He shuddered at the picture of himself facing Meyers. He could not delude himself. Every vision of the man but mocked him the more, and more frightened him. He could not escape. Everywhere he looked, the range boss's hateful face was in front of him.

A hand touched the door, and Ames

whirled, his features livid.

Tara stood in the doorway.

A snarling relief burst out of him
Straightening, he mopped his flushed cheeks
'Well?' he blustered. 'What're you staring at!

She came into the room, pulling the door
shut behind her. 'How did you ever get into
such a mess?'

Scowling, he flung himself into a chair. He
eyes made him squirm.

'I warned you, Holly. Where were you
going?'

'What difference does that make?'

'Why did he take the horse away from you?
She said, impatiently, '*Why did you let him*?'

He continued to glare.

'Get up and do something!' She said
exasperated: 'Where's your pride?'

He sprang to his feet, all outrage and fury
'I'll handle this!'

'You've got to do it right now.'

Going over to the bureau, she pulled open a
drawer, and turned, holding out Mike'
cartridge belt and pistol. Ames backed away
from them.

'Put it on,' Tara said, 'and go out there and
fire him.'

CHAPTER FOURTEEN

'Are you crazy!'

The girl stared a good while at him. 'Unless you face Meyers down, you'll have to clear out—'

'So that's your game,' he cried with a sneer. 'With this ranch in your pocket, I'm no longer important!'

'I didn't say that.'

'You ain't fooling me none.' Some of Ames' fury got into his voice. 'You'll find out how important I am! That feller will take this place plumb away from you!'

'Jock?' Tara said. 'What's happening to us— what's the matter with you? Can't you understand what you let loose out there? Being owner of a spread carries responsibilities ... obligations, I suppose Sheriff Tolliver would call them. A kind of code. Not to be shirked or side-stepped.'

She considered him gravely. 'There's power in Star Circle—called up by the strength of the people who ride for it. This works for us, but only so long as every man measures up. Meyers made you look ridiculous. If it goes any further, the whole range will be laughin'.' She looked at him fiercely. 'You've *got* to get rid of him.'

'What you want is to get me killed!'

Someone pounded on the door.

Tara scowled. 'Yes?'

Jace Lathram, it appeared, had just driven up.

'Ask him in,' Tara said. 'We'll be right along. Fetch cakes and wine—the port, I think.' She regarded Ames darkly. 'Tell Meyers to come, too.'

When the servant had gone, Ames cried bitterly, 'You must think I haven't an ounce of sense!'

'I'll wear the outfit you got me at More Oaks,' she said. 'Here—help me off with this blouse.'

'I'm not going out there. That son of a bitch!'

'He's come to read the will,' Tara said, struggling out of the blouse. 'That's why I want Meyers to sit in on this.' She got into the dress and stepped across to the mirror, passing a brush through her hair. 'Do I look all right?'

Ames glared, watching her tuck in the bright gleam of stray locks.

'It's the best chance you'll have.' She smoothed the cloth over her hips, shook out the skirt. 'Jock won't try anything in front of Lathram. We'll have the banker as witness that you fired him. Strap on that pistol and pull yourself together.'

In an anguish of indecision he followed her white-cheeked and muttering, down the hall.

*   *   *

The hand from Star Circle found Benton Pearce, but the parson wasn't able to set out straightaway. He doubted Tara's need of him was based on anything more urgent than a desire to conform with what was expected of her. From a long acquaintanceship with the frailties of suffering humanity, Pearce no longer looked for miracles.

He had found people pretty much the same everywhere, once the bluster and pretenses were stripped from what they told you. They were set in motion and hounded by a conglomeration of alarms and cravings. The girl's life had not been easy. Confronted with what she undoubtedly felt to be a continual round of unvaried drudgery, he was not surprised she had been taken in by the urbane and personable Ames. Pearce had sadly foreseen this when he'd found her that evening outside Ames' door. He wondered how long she would put up with the man.

He watched the sun in a red blaze of glory slip behind the blue-black peaks. He'd learned to take things as he found them, with a kind of dry humor that generally permitted him to strike a fair balance between what was and what his calling insisted had ought to be.

He wasn't given to snap judgments. He tried to bring out the best in a person, though he had not always been God's man; and sometimes, even in spite of his training, he was prone to let temper engulf him.

It was dark when he picked up the lights of
Star Circle.

*   *   *

The banker took Tara's hands, bending over
them.

'Mr Lathram, this is my husband,' she said.
'Hollister Ames, of St Louis.'

The men briefly nodded. The banker's look
under white tufts of brows, moved over Ames
and as quickly dismissed him. 'Turning colder'
he said. 'Wouldn't be surprised if that wind
fetched snow.'

In the thickening quiet of Ames' angry flush
Jock Meyers arrived, the heavy tramp of his
boots coming over the gallery floor. He flung
open the door, coming in with the gale, and
shoved it shut, settling his shoulders solidly
against it.

'You know Mike's range boss,' Tara said to
the banker. They nodded. 'Have some of these
cakes, a glass of wine—Mike used to say this
port would take the paint off a plowshare.'

Lathram waved it away. 'I have to get back.'
He got out a pair of steel-rimmed spectacles
held them to the light, huffed a few times, and
proceeded to give them a careful polishing.
'This may come,' he said, 'as something of a
shock. Mike didn't leave a will. Never made
one.'

'No will!' Tara gasped.

104

Lathram shook his head. 'Mike wasn't a man to spend thought on dying. Too alive to the present, too secure in his judgments ever to imagine a time they might not bind folks. However, as next of kin, his closest blood relative, you'll come in for everything he had, of course.' The banker, pursing his lips, regarded her earnestly. 'I must advise you to sell at least a part of this ranch.'

The stillness stretched. Ames' lid-narrowed eyes were like two pieces of glass, and the range boss, Meyers, moved his cud to the other cheek.

Tara said, 'I don't understand.'

'Takes cash to run a ranch.' Lathram sighed. 'To face the hard facts, all you've got in the bank is two hundred dollars and forty-three cents.'

Ames' mouth was pinched. The range boss grinned. Tara's chin came up. 'That doesn't seem likely.' She cried indignantly: 'He must have had more than that! All the herds he sold—'

'We've had two years of drought and three years of nothing but rain,' the banker said. 'Last herd he sold was on a mighty poor market. He's always fancied a big crew, and big crews wade through cash like a hungry dog goin' through a plate of bones. These last years more than half his help's been Mexicans. They've all got families, and ever' one of those families has been on Mike's neck. Look

105

around you,' he grumbled—'kids underfoot ever'place a man turns! What kind of way is that to run a ranch? Top of everything else, he chunked a big wad of cash into that bunch of crazy steam cars—this high-falutin railroad that was going to make Jay Goulds out of half the fools on this range!

'Don't talk to me! I say a child would know better'n to do some of the things your grandpappy did!' Lathram puffed out his cheeks. 'I didn't come here to argue. You got two hundred dollars. You got what cows are packin' his brand, and that top-heavy crew. You can't ship cattle and get more'n their cost in freight ... You might ship some of that grass if 'twas baled. In drought areas, now, you might get enough for it to tide you over if you had a little time—which you haven't. Chalkchild's gone to the Indian Agent, swelled up bigger'n a frog with the gout—claims they haven't been paid in two years.'

He put his glasses away. 'You better sell some of this range. I'm not saying the sodbusters'll buy ... But you got to turn loose of something. You'd better do it quick!'

'Then we'll get rid of the Mexicans,' Tara said. 'I'm not going to break this ranch up.'

The white tufts on the banker's eyes sprang up. 'Ain't, eh? Well! Maybe the folks up in Washin'ton'll do it. Now, you listen to me—'

'Just a moment.' Ames stepped forward. 'Star Circle's not in debt to the bank here, I

106

take it?'

'To the bank?' Lathram's brows came down above a look at the range boss. He tugged at the whiskers growing out of his chin. 'No ... But the bank can't loan no money to a woman, if that's what you're gettin' at.'

Tara's cheeks darkened. Before she could unleash her anger, Ames cut in suavely: 'I don't believe your bank could swing the kind of deal I have in mind. If you have things straight the place is in pretty deep—'

'Too deep to pull out,' the banker said harshly.

Ames smiled. He could do this well, particularly when, as now, he was figuring to buy time. 'Afraid I can't agree with you. This ranch has an ocean of grass. That grass can be utilized. With a little refinancing—'

'You talk like a fool! No one,' Lathram snapped, 'is goin' to throw good money after bad. Not with that mob of land-hungry grangers bustin' to swarm all over this place!'

'Oh, I don't know,' Ames said. 'You pointed out yourself we've got plenty of manpower. I'm connected with a firm that might see Star Circle in a different light—as a place,' he said smugly, 'to fatten up steers hauled out of drought areas. Crimp, Crane and Cranston might go for a deal like this. On a long-term mortgage, with nothing to pay the first year but interest and with culls staving off the squawks of those Indians, I think my wife might do

107

rather well.'

Lathram's expression was one of balked greed and rage. He scrambled into his coat and snatched up his hat. He said straight out, 'I'll give twenty thousand dollars for this spread just like it stands!'

'Mr Lathram,' Ames chuckled, 'you astonish and confound me. I'm sure this comes right out of your heart, but I'm afraid Mrs Ames has made the position quite clear.'

Lathram turned fishbelly white. Tara, alive with renewed hope and confidence, looked approvingly at Ames. The range boss, snorting, got out of the banker's way.

Whirling, Lathram said, 'Don't come whining to me when the St Louis packers put you out of this place!'

Yanking open the door, he stomped violently out.

Ames, belatedly trapped with his own smartness, wondered where he would be if the banker decided to get in touch with the packing house. Perspiring, he failed completely to notice Jock Meyers quit the room.

Ames tried to push away his worrisome fears. It shouldn't require more than a handful of hours to line up the suckers and cram the cash into his carpetbags.

Squaring padded shoulders, he was startled to find his wife eyeing him darkly. 'You were saying, my dear?' He dragged a smile across his teeth.

It appeared to infuriate her. 'What do you think I gave you that gun for!'

Ames stared at her blankly.

'*Meyers!*' she cried. 'What's the matter with you? Why didn't you do what I told you? Why did you let him slip out of here that way?'

Ames, jaws clamped, walked out of the room.

CHAPTER FIFTEEN

Star Circle had gone to her head. All that yap about responsibility, and then coming out with *We'll get rid of the Mexicans!* Only two days ago she'd been glad to have hold of him; now all she could think about was getting him killed!

Ames damned Jock Meyers, but the man's cold face was in his mind like a cancer.

Only chance for a stake lay in More Oaks where those plow chasers were talking up a storm. They wouldn't all be strapped. Some of them had probably sold out businesses to come here. He'd get off this place if he had to hoof it!

He stopped in the gloom-filled hall to stand bitterly, vindictively, listening. The goddam place was still as a coffin.

He stood gnawing his lip. It graveled him to think of slipping away with empty pockets. There ought to be something he could trade for

109

hard cash. Straight ahead on the left was Mike's office.

He listened for Tara. Undecided, he crept nearer the dark hole of the office. Blacker in there than the gut of a cat.

Somewhere outside he heard the dog bark. With a last look around he sidled into the room.

For an eternity he stood crouched like a rabbit, ears stretched, tense with excitement. With infinite care he eased the door shut. Not daring to risk a light, even now, he tried to remember the placement of the furnishings. A table off there against that wall between windows. Here a leather chair and, back of it, the hat rack. Desk would be straight ahead.

He put out a hand, cautiously feeling his way. Just as he touched a flat surface, the dog broke into a hellish racket of barking.

Ames froze. He heard a jumble of calls and the hoofs of a horse coming into the yard. Sweat clammed his hands. *How was he going to get past that dog!*

He began to sift through the contents of pigeonholes, encountering nothing which felt like currency. He got the wide center drawer out, stealthily hunting for a hidden compartment.

Pausing frequently to listen, he was in the third drawer when some warning yanked his head around. The door he'd so carefully shut stood open.

110

Her husband was a coward.

Tara faced it squarely. He would never get rid of Jock Meyers. He'd be all the time finding excuses. How he'd managed, at More Oaks, to knock down Joe Wheeler ... Well! She could see plain enough he'd be no help against Meyers.

But Meyers had to go.

Star Circle was hers, and it was going to stay hers. She hadn't got out from under Mike's shadow to give in now to the whims of Mike's range boss. She was not going to have a man around who wouldn't take orders.

She went suddenly still. That strange rider ... that beard-stubbled redhead who'd come up to watch Ames put the saddle back. Why did he seem so peculiarly familiar?

Of course! He was the one who'd got off with his warsack at Stroud—the cowboy who'd told Ames about Mike and Mike's cattle. The rusty-faced one...

They were *her* cattle now!

She remembered the flat hard shine of his eyes looking back at Ames from the Lone Star's veranda; and she heard the dog bark.

A horse came clop-clopping into the yard. Voices lifted out of the dark. All at once Tara realized the preacher was out there, and she sprang up, filled with confusion.

Angry, impatient, still in a flutter, she hauled

open the door, stepping onto the gallery. 'What's the trouble out there?'

At first, no one answered. Saddle leather skreaked. 'Some jasper...' Meyers' growl reached out of the wind. 'Claims his name's Pearce.'

'Send him over.' She tried to fight down her panic. The man would have to spend the night. She said, 'See to his horse,' and moved inside, trying desperately to ridicule the threat of him away. She was Tara Drood with three hundred thousand acres of grass!

Now why, she wondered, going abruptly still, hadn't she called herself Mrs Hollister Ames? Was she already, in her own mind, renouncing ... She heard him move across the gallery; his hand was against the door.

'Come in!' she gasped.

He stood holding his hat, heavy-shouldered and grave, with the wind tumbling his silver-streaked hair. His eyes reached across to her again the way they had that night outside Ames' room. 'I come soon's I could.'

Blood pounded into her cheeks. The walls seemed to sway and quiver. Lord, but he was big! She couldn't imagine him acting with Meyers the way Ames had.

She tried to gain control of her voice. 'Wasn't no cause for you to break your fool neck. Buryin' ain't till tomorrow.' She tried to meet his stare. She smoothed her dress about her hips. 'I expect you'll be minded,' she said,

112

'to set up with him,' and wheeled off toward the hall, not quite running but wanting to.

'Kind of aimed,' he said, 'to talk with you a little.'

'With ... *me?*' She went still, feeling trapped, too scared to look around.

'You're Mike's nearest. What you need is someone handy to kind of wool things around with. Won't you sit down?'

She hated this, *hated* it. She didn't want to be in the room with him, even. If she could, she would have put the whole length of Star Circle ... The horsehair sofa came against her legs and she let herself gingerly down on the edge of it.

'You'll be leavin', I suppose, soon's you get the ranch sold?'

Sold! Sell Star Circle. Her hackles shot up, and she came sharply around. 'I hadn't figured to sell. Were you layin' out to buy?'

The barbed shaft of her malice evidently went past him. He was enormously astonished. 'You're not figurin' to *run* it!'

'You tryin' to make out I'm stupid?'

Pearce's stare slanched around. He scrubbed a hand across his mouth. 'Now, just a minute—'

'If you'd done half what I've done around this ... and don't say nothing about me bein' a *girl!*'

Pearce backed away, his flush more pronounced as she came up, starting after him.

113

'Whoa up there, now!' he cried. 'Easy does it...'

He might have been talking to a recalcitrant bronc, so deceptively soothing, so persuasive was his voice. 'Ain't nobody tryin' to auger you out...'

But he was not fooling Tara. They were all the same, never willing to give a woman credit for anything. She glared 'Don't say another word!'

'Ma'am, I surely won't,' he declared, watchfully. 'Star Circle's yours—I wouldn't try to say different. Only thing...' His voice wizzled off. He hauled in a deep breath. 'You keepin' this crew? No harm askin' that, is there?'

'Depends why you're asking. Why *are* you?'

'Well, there's other people to be thought of—whole families,' Pearce said. 'What happens to Star Circle's goin' to affect every one of them.'

'I sent for you to bury Old Mike. When the dirt rattles onto his box, you'll be paid. These "families,"' Tara said, 'they'll be away from here directly.' She gave him a hard look and headed for the door.

'You got a moral duty to them Mex'kins, ma'am. You can't just heave 'em out—'

'I've had one lecture tonight. I'm not goin' to stand here listening to another!'

She yanked open the door and stormed into the hall.

114

Pearce shook his head. There was good in this girl. A deep inner beauty that warmed him like a flame. Everything was against her: the times, her background, the pressures of environment, lack of experience, her own youth and the passions indigenous to it.

Pearce saw these things, and beyond them the glory. Here was a fine bold soul at the crossroads. With her yellow hair and those angry eyes, Tara Drood was a challenge.

*   *   *

In the office, Ames froze, eyes on that open door.

He would have sworn he had closed it. All the dread possibilities went coldly through him. Who was crouched in this blackness, watching him, waiting...

Not Tara, he felt sure, and it wasn't Meyers. They'd have spoken. One of the servants? Would he feel the cold rip of a knife if he moved?

But he couldn't stay here! He cringed, skin crawling. No telling what might happen if he were discovered here by Tara. He began to shake.

In sudden panic he lunged, snarling, toward the lesser dark of the gloom-filled hall. There he pulled up to peer back, sweating, feeling like a fool.

Anger began to boil up, a kind of murderous

115

hate compounded of the things he'd been subjected to here. Then he was staring, eyes bulging, locked in his tracks by sheer incredulity. The door was moving, stealthily closing. He would not believe it until he heard the latch click.

Like Ichabod Crane, he fled, running blindly.

In the office a cackling old woman was bent double with laughter.

CHAPTER SIXTEEN

Ames appeared hopelessly lost in a labyrinth of shacks.

Winded, bewildered, he was furious enough, frustrated enough, to have tackled Jock Meyers with bare hands had they met. Nothing like this had ever happened before and he could not understand how the closing of a door could so thoroughly have stampeded him.

Shaking with anger he glared into the windy dark. He made out the open hole of a doorway, saw the flapping blur of what looked like a skirt and, beyond, a solid blackness lifting into the night that could be nothing less than a sheer wall of rock.

The cliff!

Ames wheeled, cursing. He was back of the house—how far he didn't know, but well

116

behind that clutter of pens.

Sounds began to leach through the roar of his blood ... a child's screams of temper, the soothing mumble of a woman, a man's impatient tones. Guitar music floated on the swirls of the wind, and Ames discovered the gray shape of the barn distantly south against a halo of light that must be coming from the ranch house.

His first anxious impulse was to head for the horse trap, but remembrance came with its vision of Meyers. If it was the ramrod's purpose to keep Ames here the man would have posted guards.

He scowled into the wind while fear and hate churned his frustrated passions and fury chewed at the stays of caution. He took hold of Mike's gun. The hard feel of it encouraged his battered confidence.

He beat on a door, hammering loudly. 'Quién es?' a man's voice called—'what passes?'

'Open up!' Ames growled. 'Get me a horse. Straight away!'

The fellow stared at him stupidly. 'A horse, señor?'

'Caballo!' Ames shouted. 'Andale—pronto!'

'Yes...' The fellow licked at cracked lips, eyes rolling uneasily.

'I am the new patrón!' Ames cried arrogantly.

'I cannot help you, señor. These segundo she's say "Een the night no one go"—comprendez? These hombre muy malo.' His hand made the Sign.

Ames had dealt with pelados before. He brought out his wallet, but the man backed away. 'No, no, señor—' The rest was a garble of frightened Spanish. The vaquero put both hands behind him, and his woman, springing forward, slammed the door in Ames' face.

The child let out a wail of renewed crying. Ames, snarling obscenities, made for another door. A serape-clad shape rose up out of the shadows, a huge bull of a man, bigger even than Meyers with his gun on. The man anchored himself, arms akimbo, in front of Ames. 'Yes?'

Ames stopped, breath rasping louder.

'Go away! Vamanos!' a woman screamed shrilly. 'Are we fools, to steal for another what we would not take for our own? Qué paso?'

All around Ames could see men craning their necks, could catch the growl of their muttering. The big one said, 'Basta—enough! Hold your tongues!' His eyes took up Ames with an obvious contempt. 'We are of this place. I am Domatilio, foreman of vaqueros. A loyal man,' he said with quiet pride. 'For the girl I might do this; for an extranjero—a foreigner, never!' He flung out an arm. 'Go, man! Get out of my sight,' he said with disgust.

118

*　　　*　　　*

Draped with a sheet, Mike lay on his bed between flaring candles. Pearce wanted to get through to the girl's better self, but her face was stubbornly set.

'You may bury Old Mike, but no one,' Pearce said, 'ever succeeds in burying conscience. It's the invisible strand by which God in—'

'I don't have to listen to that!'

She flounced around, flushed and resentful, to show him a back as stiff as a pikestaff. Willful and foolish and proud and pathetic ... where was it all going to end? Yet she was more to be pitied than scorned, Pearce thought, more child than woman, stubbornly believing that if she would not see the things she disliked, they would inevitably disappear. But this was no harmless little-girl game. These were dangerous years, and she was playing with other people's lives. If she was old enough to climb into a bed, she was old enough to be responsible.

'Believe me, Tara, in the quietest watches of the night God will find you. No one is smart enough to hide from Him, or from the things He expects of us. If you step into your grandfather's boots, you also inherit his problems, the responsibilities—'

'They never caught up with Mike that I've noticed!'

119

Pearce said, 'Didn't they?' He was minded to shake her. 'I expect you've heard of the Wind River trouble ... of Murphy and Dolan and what happened at Lincoln—are you hankering to see that kind of thing here?'

The rebellious cant of her head was an angering reminder of her grandfather's ways. Pearce tried to remember that she'd spent all her life on this ranch ... the harshness of all that had molded her. He said, with strained patience, 'Do these farmers, this unrest, mean nothing at all?'

'I won't have you preachin' at me!' she cried. '*I* didn't make the railroad! *I* didn't bring these plow chasers here! I've got rights *too*—I'll do what I want with this place!'

There was too much at stake for a man to stand back while she plunged the country neck deep into fury—the guns would bark soon enough.

'Would you see people die just to have your own way!'

Lord, how she hated him! She tried to get past him. He shoved an arm out and caught her. 'You may not like it,' he said, yanking her around, 'but you'll listen!'

It was like trying to hang onto a wildcat. She scratched and bit. He had to wrap both arms about her and even then, with his face hot as fire, she got away from him. Panting, wild-eyed, furious, her teeth bared, she rammed a knee into his crotch and dived through the

120

door when his arms fell away.

Pearce staggered, catching hold of a chair while the pain twisted through him. The parson swore. What damnfool thing was she up to now! Maybe, he thought, he should of gone at her differently, pretending to agree until—until what? She was just like her grandfather, determined to have her own way!

Pearce dragged some air into him, clammy with sweat, still trembling all over. She'd got the bit in her teeth for fair now, he reckoned. He eased himself into a chair, dragging a sleeve across his cheeks. He tried to shut away the frightening visions, but a man couldn't be optimistic with a headstrong slip of a girl at the helm of the biggest outfit in the country.

No use looking for help from Ames. The man was plainly out of his depth; and Pearce wryly reckoned he himself was in the same bind. Never had he felt so frustratingly inadequate.

He had to go on, find a way if he could. A whole range might be hanging on what happened here. Too many hair-triggered have-nots had their sights turned this way to be cowed or held back by any chit of a girl from land that belonged to whoever could grab it.

He'd been aiming to point this out, make it plain to her. He might better, he guessed, have come straight out with it. He should have told her these were *people* she was dealing with, not just a bunch of black marks on some tally

sheet. Flesh-and-blood people, like hersel
that were fed to the gills with being shove
around. This was what he ought to have tol
her. Coming into power had gone to her heac
She'd got her tail up now, a-whickerin an
snorting like a stallion bronc. About all
man—

One shot, then another crashing right on it
heels, flattened over the yard and hit the front
of the buildings.

Pearce sprang up and ran through the house

He saw them as he opened the front door
they were fanned out, statue still, in the butter
yellow light from the bunkhouse windows–
the whole crew, it looked like.

Whatever had happened was over and done

Moving through the stiff silence, he foun
what their shocked stares were fixed on, th
crumpled thing on the ground that had bee
Jock Meyers. A glance told Pearce the ma
would never get up.

He took in the pointed gun with the smok
still dribbling blue from its snout, and the ma
who held it. Pearce eyed the sardonic twist o
rusty cheeks, the coppery shine of red bristles

'Well, Fludd?'

The pale eyes stared back unwinking. Flud
was not to be talked into anything. 'Ask her,
he said with a jerk of his chin.

The girl pulled her look off Meyers with
shiver. She seemed, Pearce thought, unable t
believe the man was dead. Her voice sounde

flat, almost mechanical, as though what she said was a recitation: 'I told Meyers to get rid of the Mexicans. He refused. I told him he was fired and'—she looked bewildered—'he laughed. He just stood there and laughed.' A flush crept over her cheeks. Her chin came up in that gesture Pearce remembered. 'I asked if anyone else wanted the job, and this fellow spoke up. "It's yours," I told him, "if you can handle this crew." Meyers began swearing. He grabbed at his pistol.'

Pearce could see that this was logical.

Fludd's bleach-eyed look swiveled over the crew. 'All right. You heard. Git on back to your knittin'.'

'Getting rid of folks,' Pearce said, 'is about the likeliest thing you do, isn't it, Fludd?'

'I ain't heard no complaints.' Watching the crew drift away, Fludd slipped the big gun back into his belt.

'Aren't you going to carve a notch for him?'

Fludd considered Pearce coldly, impersonal as a snake. 'I leave that for the suckers.' He said to the girl, 'You still wantin' them Mexkins moved off the place?'

Tara found Pearce's eyes upon her, and she tightened up. 'I sure do! Right after the buryin'!'

'I'll pass the word along.' Fludd grinned. 'I don't look for there to be no trouble.'

Tara headed for the house.

About all a man could do, Pearce guessed,

was try to keep in sight and maybe pick up some of the pieces.

CHAPTER SEVENTEEN

She'd got her grandfather planted and she'd got Meyers out of her hair. She wouldn't hear of putting him up there with Mike, but had a couple of the hands pack him clean off Star Circle. As if, having scrubbed the blood of him off her hands, she wanted nothing left around to remind her of the man. Fludd had given out the orders, but no one doubted they had come straight from her.

She hadn't taken any guff from the neighbors. Everybody and his uncle, just about, had shown up, most of them bulging with pious platitudes, but some, bolder perhaps or harder pressed, were fretting and fuming to call for a new deal. They might as well have saved themselves the ride. Soon as she'd got the old man into the ground, Tara had gone off and shut herself up in the house. Nobody felt much encouragement to linger, not with that gun fighter standing around like some overgrown vulture, thumbs hooked into the brass shine of his belt. Most of that bunch could take a plain hint, particular when it appeared, as now, to be the last frail thing between themselves and a case of rigor mortis.

Pearce, standing near, watched the exodus in silence. He had the conviction he was witnessing the end of an era. There were plenty of hard looks and dark mutterings, but nobody pulled over to brace the new boss. Fludd stood with a saturnine grin on his face, watching Mike's Mexicans begin their long walk.

Here again, Pearce reflected, though despair and anger didn't have to be hunted for, no one looked about to take issue with Fludd. One puff of black powder had put the man in the saddle, his authority established, a travesty of justice.

It was an embittering sight: women toting babies and whatever else they might carry, trudging off up the road through the blowing lemon dust and the swirling smoke of the burning possessions too awkward to carry; old women with tears streaming down their cheeks, toil-bent, some of them gnarled as junipers, most of them barefoot; the bewildered faces of their men trudging beside them, some gripping rifles.

Pearce was minded to saddle up and get away from the ranch, but conscience wouldn't let him. He'd got to try again to awaken some sense of responsibility in the girl, some realization of what she was laying up for herself. That there was more to this than could be reasonably bounded by the strict confines of his own obligations was a possibility Pearce refused to consider. He was determined to have his say if he were forced to camp out at this spread all winter.

During the next ten days it began to look as if he might have to. Tara, it became apparent, was deliberately avoiding him. She took her meals in her room, seldom appearing when he was around, never permitting herself to be alone with him. Twice he attempted to speak in front of Ames, but the girl adroitly managed on both occasions to avoid him.

On the seventh day it snowed.

For hours the falling flakes formed an impenetrable curtain, shutting Star Circle away from the world. Then a wind sprang up and gloomily cried about the eaves. The temperature dropped. The outside cold crept into the buildings. Inside the house what few servants were left moodily huddled about the great fires they'd built up with logs dragged in by the half-frozen crew.

All the riders were out, their hours divided by Fludd between hauling wood and scattering hay for the bunched-up cattle standing around through the hills, forlornly bawling.

It snowed off and on for the next three days, and the men, blue-cheeked and half blinded, worked in shifts around the clock. Pearce went out too, doing what he could. The feed had to be hauled on sled wagons now, and in some places even these couldn't get through. They had four horses hitched to each huge sled, with an extra team breaking track ahead. It was

126

grueling work in the bitter wind. Patience ran thin, and tempers became shorter as the snow crusted over in the deepening cold.

The snow finally quit, and on the ninth night a thaw set in and the mercury at last climbed back into sight.

It was on the next morning that Pearce had his say.

*   *   *

All this while Ames had been moping about the house, glaring and swearing, growing hourly more impossible, more crossgrained and caustic. Hardly a subject could be mentioned that did not draw some snide remark from him.

Tara found very little about her husband during this period to stir up feelings of admiration or pride. He was beginning to get under her skin with his continual grumblings of having to get to town. 'If you miss More Oaks so fierce,' she said once, 'why not pack up your coats and your collars and go there?' Fed up with everything about him, after his next show of temper she locked him out of their room. Let him go to his trashy women! The plans she was nursing had no place for a tinhorn.

Her mind fairly teemed with ambitious schemes. Penny-proud—that was Mike, all right. He hadn't even begun to see the possibilities that had surrounded him. There

127

was no end to the things Star Circle might accomplish, given someone with guts and vision to shape its course. What was good in having all this—the toughest crew, the biggest spread, the hardest goddam riders in the country, the hundreds of thousands of unplowed acres—if you weren't going to get some use from them? All her years she'd been used. Now she meant to get some use out of others!

She wasn't shelving her plans just because some pry-eyed preacher had to poke his long nose into the deal. Though she'd kept out of his way, Pearce had frequently, hatefully, been in her thoughts. Frowning, and all puffed up with his righteousness—and him no more than a draggletail devil chaser! Did he think that by hanging around like this he was going to keep her from putting this ranch on its feet?

To get the kind of life she'd envisioned for herself, Star Circle had to be saved, and she had made a good start by getting rid of Mike's Mexicans. Pound-foolish, that banker had called Mike. Thinking back, she was forced to agree. Keeping up all those pelados! One way or another she would pay off the Indians and make Star Circle impregnable. What was needed was a few prime examples, and Tara didn't reckon she'd have to look far.

Bright and early the morning after the thaw had set in, she was out in the yard bundled up like an Eskimo when the crew, shrugging into their coats, came straggling from the cookshack.

She beckoned Fludd over. 'What have you laid out for today?'

The man's glance showed a brash, even bold, approval. 'We prob'ly taken considerable loss in that storm. Cows was driftin' pretty bad them first days,' he said, buttoning the heavy windbreaker over his bony chest. 'Figured the boys better comb out some of them draws—'

'That can wait.' Tara broke off to stare, annoyed, when the preacher came over and took root within arm's reach. 'Well?'

'Go right ahead,' Pearce said in that aggravating drawl that never failed to get up her hackles. 'I expect my business can wait till you get finished.'

Tara's eyes turned coldly angry, almost, it might have seemed, as though he put her out of countenance. Pearce took this for a hopeful sign. Perhaps all his words hadn't fallen on stony ground. The conscience he'd warned her of was beginning to make itself felt, he guessed, and smiled.

'You go right ahead,' he said again, meeting the challenge of Fludd's displeasure with the same offhand agreeableness. 'I got plenty of time.'

Tara turned her back on him. The man was insufferable. She couldn't stand out in this cold all day. She said tightly to Fludd, 'You know that batch of squatters that's dug in up around

Twin Peaks?'

'That Bar 7 tribe—them LeGrues, you mean?'

'They're the main ones.' Tara nodded. 'Might be some others settled in by now. I want them choused out of there, lock, stock, and—'

'Wait a minute!' Pearce said. 'You can't run those people off that land. That's government range—'

'It's Star Circle grass!' Tara flared, wheeling around.

'But Mike—'

'*I'm* running Star Circle.'

'Be reasonable, girl! What *harm* are they doing?'

'They're a signpost for others.' She turned back to Fludd. 'I want them out. Right now! Take the crew up there and get at it.'

'Yes, *ma'am!*' Fludd grinned. This was more like it. Good for the crew, too. Put some ginger in them. He let his saturnine stare scratch across Pearce's cheeks, and hitched up his gun belt. 'We'll git straight at it.' His look sent the jingler flying after the horse herd. 'We'll hit them weedbenders like a dose of Black 40. You're wantin' a clean sweep, that right?'

'You deef or something?'

'Just fixin' to make sure.' The glint of wicked laughter gleamed in Fludd's eyes as his lizard-cold stare met Pearce's. 'Just figurin' to git the straight of things.'

'Burn them out,' Tara said stonily. 'Don't

130

leave one rock on top of another.'

Pearce looked at the girl as if he couldn't believe it.

Pearce shook his head. 'Don't you know what will happen?'

'They should of thought about that before they grubbed out the grass. This ranch is mine. It's going to stay mine.' She said to him fiercely, 'Get off this place if you don't like what I do!'

The wrangler came back with his cavvy of fuzztails and sent them into the day pen where the crew roped out mounts and cinched up in a hurry. They climbed aboard with their rifles. Pearce watched them ride out. He turned back to the girl.

The pity she found in his face was intolerable. She flung up her head, crying at him, furious: 'I will do whatever I have to do! Now get off Star Circle, and stay off!'

CHAPTER EIGHTEEN

In the house, after he'd gone, in a deepening stillness Tara sat grayly staring at walls across which the tangled skeins of her thoughts bleakly swirled in half glimpsed fragments. Remembering the sad look of the More Oaks preacher, in a rage she let fly with the hairbrush, and then peered, strangely frightened, at the gouge of flaked plaster.

131

With knuckles squeezed against white teeth, she whirled to stare into the mirror, groping to understand herself. Where was the satisfaction she'd thought to find as mistress of Mike's acres?

She stared in uncomprehending fascination at the eyes peering out of her tousled mop of wheatstraw hair. Was this Tara Drood? Was this *really* her?

She fled, spinning in a flutter of skirts, to catch at the door and stand breathless, listening into a deep, pulsating stillness.

Where was everybody? Where was Ames? Jesusita?

She flung open the door, crept down the long hall with the echoing footsteps hurrying behind her, stopping when she stopped, then starting up again, stealthily brittle as bits of crunched glass.

Somewhere the dog barked, its climbing yammer breaking off in full cry. Tara blindly ran, ran until the kitchen's gray cavern closed about her. Seeing nothing but emptiness, her panic mounted. With her eyes wildly raking the curdle of shadows, a crackle of breath reached out like a slap and, like a slap, restored her.

Muy borracho—drunk again!

She stared at her mother in a horror of revulsion. Jesusita might have been some old witch with her toothless gums, pipestem arms and beady eyes. There was something unnerving, almost *unclean*, about the way the old woman sat cackling into the clatterous stillness. Like those sly looks of Ames', Pearce's unwanted compassion, it disturbed Tara, angering her.

What was wrong with them—all of them? Why was Jesusita always drunk anymore? What was it that seemed so ugly to Tara, finding her mother all alone here, and laughing?

'Are you cold?' she asked. 'Shall I build up the fire?'

'It is always cold.' The old woman shivered, tightly hugging herself. The black eyes flicked about, and again a cackle came from the red hole of her mouth. 'A-a-ai-hé! I told you. You will never get more from a cat than its hide!'

Tara looked her impatience. 'What nonsense is this?'

'That gringo—the one you took off your clothes for. Did I not tell you he was a robber?'

'Ames?'

'Did you warm your thighs with someone else, then?'

Tara glared. She cried, cheeks hot, 'I am legally married—'

'And a fool!' the old woman cackled. 'As great a fool as your father, who let this place destroy him. Do you imagine I can't see? Your head is like a window. Will you kill the foreigner—is that why he is afraid, why he runs from a closing door?'

'I don't know what you are talking about.'

'Where is Meyers? Why is this red one giving the orders—'

'*I* give the orders—'

'May the devil be deaf.' The old woman rocked herself. The silence pressed in, the skreaks of her chair sawing across it like gagging. The beady eyes dug at Tara. 'Where have you sent those rifles?'

'I know what I'm doing.' Tara tossed her head.

She went out of the room, but the cackle followed her. 'Your father said that. And where is he now?'

'He was killed by a horse!'

'Does it make any difference how you're killed when you are dead?'

Catching up her skirts, Tara ran as from the conscience Pearce had hung about her neck. Down the echoing hall, past rows of closed doors and into the living room's wealth of bright sunlight she fled. Its solid walls shut out her fears. When she stopped, breathless, she was again her own mistress.

Pride came into the line of her jaw. Her features tightened. She laughed, and flung back the tumbled heavy mop of her taffy hair. She remembered the boldness of Fludd's unguarded look, and an ache crept into the nipples of her breasts. She found it hard to breathe.

A clap of sound, sharply frightening, jerked her round. Eyes wide, she stared at the open hall door. No hand had touched it, no wind had slammed it, yet sound was there like a broken stick ... *like a pistol shot!*

She ran out into the glare of the empty yard, on toward the stark peeled poles of the pens. She saw the dead dog.

Fear rose up and filled her throat. Nowhere was there motion yet the dog was dead. She saw the blood welling out of its mouth, and pressed both hands against her temples.

Badly shaken she returned to the house. She got Mike's rifle from its corner, jacking it open to make sure of the loads. She closed the breech and sank down by the door, all the old frustrations congealing inside her. She tried to will the crew to come back from Twin Peaks, yet knew they could not return before morning. A sick loneliness twisted the things in her head. Almost on the back of her neck she could feel the man's breath. *Where was he?* Was he stalking her now or hiding, waiting? Perhaps in one of those hovels beyond the corrals from which Fludd had driven Mike's brood of Mexicans?

And where was Ames?

Her red lips curled when she thought of the man she had set so much store by. It did not occur to her that Ames was the killer.

*　　　*　　　*

Ames, hidden in one of those emptied houses,

had watched Fludd and the crew ride out, thinking that here was his chance. Horses had been left in the day pen; he could see them, head to rump, restlessly stomping, flinging their heads as though sampling the wind that was beginning to roughen.

It was the best chance he was likely to get. He thought of Tara, not afraid of her, yet unable to put his nervousness aside. She was a strong-willed woman. He was aware that if he left, she would never take him back, and was bothered by the nagging conviction that she might be just bitch enough to pull this off, to take hold and hang onto this place regardless.

He finally made up his mind. Down on all fours he crept in among the pens. There were five sets of poles between himself and the horses. Having no idea where Fludd had gone, getting a horse took a longer time than he cared to devote to it, and he was reluctant to put himself in view of the ranch-house windows.

Fear of discovery put a lather of sweat on him. His temper turned ugly. Twice he blundered into cactus, trying to keep an eye on the house. Not having seen Pearce leave, he was gnawed by worry, scared the preacher was on the gallery with Tara. He scarcely noticed the pain of his lacerated hands. When the dog reared up in front of him, barking, Ames grabbed out a knife. When the brute leaped he ripped the blade through its belly. The dog fell rolled, but managed to drag itself up. Ames panicked now, saw the snarling teeth within two feet of him. He snatched his gun out and fired pointblank.

He was more frightened then. He had visions of men pouring out of the bunkhouse, of Pearce and the girl rushing in to cut him off. He jumped up and blindly ran, not toward the horses but crazily away from them, expecting every moment to hear Pearce yell, to be caught in a cross fire.

With the breath sawing terribly in and out of his near-bursting lungs he dived into the cover of the abandoned houses, and collapsed.

*   *   *

Tara jerked up her head, not sure what had awakened her. The big room was thick with shadows. She got up. Through the partly open front door she could see, in the lesser gloom of the yard, the shifting mounted shape of a big-hatted rider half bent over, peering, just beyond the dark posts of the gallery.

'Hello in there—anybody home?'

The girl poked the barrel of a Winchester at him. 'Stop right there!'

The words came out in a cracked and frightened whisper. But the man must have glimpsed the dull shine of the rifle. He held the horse motionless. 'That you, Miz Tara?' he called, sounding nervous.

'Strike a light. I want a look at you!'

'Gawd sakes, girl, watch out fer that trigger
He got a match from his hatband, running
over the leg of his Levi's, holding up the flam
to one side of his face. 'It's on'y me, Ti
Tolliver...'

Tara's knees threatened to unhinge, so vas
was her relief. She couldn't have put into word
what she'd feared, but with her terror fallin;
away a wicked anger rushed through her
'What's the marshal of More Oaks doing ou
here?'

'Wal, uh... hadn't you better mebbe ask m
to git down? I'm jest about wore to a frazzle
what with all this ridin'—'

'If you come for the buryin', it's already
over.'

With a smothered oath the man let go of hi
match. 'We got augerin' to do—you better git
lamp lit,' he growled, bringing up the hand to
blow at fried fingers.

'Star Circle's got no talking to do with any
marshal.'

'Ain't marshal no more,' he said, fixing to
get down. 'I'm sheriff of this here county. Now
where-at's that tinhorn you went an' go
yourse'f hitched up to?'

'Ames?'

'I dunno what his name is. All's I know—'

'Don't get out of that saddle!'

Tolliver stared, and edgily settled back, the
breath coming out of him in a testy grunt. 'You
better start tryin' to use a little politeness. I go

somethin' here you better take a look at afore you go settin' up play Gawd a'mighty!'

'Turn that horse an' get out of here!'

Tolliver looked at the lifted rifle and began to swell up like a bloated toad. 'You can't run off the Law like you done them damn Mex'kins! You Droods,' he shouted, 'better git it through your heads this country's all done bowin' an' scrapin' to Star Circle! Other people has got—'

'You going to argue with a bullet?'

'You wouldn't dast!' he said to her doggedly. 'I got a injunction again' this spread, an', by grannies, I aim—'

Tara squeezed the trigger. The bang of the rifle lifted the sheriff's horse off the ground, and it came down kicking like a Neuches steer. Tolliver, cursing, pitched and jerked trying to keep in touch with his saddle. When he got the animal's head up, he was shaking with rage. 'That does it!' he cried. 'I'm goin' to throw ever' goddam law in the book at you!'

Tara dropped another shot between the legs of his horse. The bronc took off like hell emigrating on cartwheels. The girl slammed the door, put her back against it, and sagged there, laughing as if she were never going to stop.

CHAPTER NINETEEN

The preacher was sitting with a stogie on the hotel veranda when the sheriff, still fuming, got back to More Oaks. A child could have sensed without half trying that Tolliver was in a real hound-kicking mood. Pearce's eyes thoughtfully followed as the lawman rode through shafts of light to climb stiffly down before the dark jail. Afterward, sighing, pinching out his cigar, frugally stowing it in his breast pocket, Pearce got up and stepped inside, minded to get out of the night's deepening chill.

He found the deserted lobby too stuffy, and went up the creaking stairs to his room. Not bothering with a lamp, he took off his clothes, chocked up the window, and tiredly stretched out on the bed's lumpy tick.

He was too disturbed for sleep to come easily. Tolliver had gone to Star Circle to serve a court order, and by the look of his face it was still in his pocket. It was an attachment meant to satisfy the claims of the Indian Agent, and it was made against Mike's estate on behalf of the Apaches in lieu of the still-unpaid lease money.

The sheriff could now do one of three things: report his failure to the court and go back out there with a posse; wash his hands of the matter; or take his troubles to the fort.

Tolliver had the look of a buck passer. But, inordinately proud of his new authority, humbled and vindictive, there was a good chance he'd go back there himself. The man, like the rest of this country, had little love for Star Circle. Pearce thought he probably would go back with a sworn-in passel of barflies and squatters.

Nothing good would come out of that. The girl was proud, too, and Fludd, with the whole weight of Star Circle back of him, would doubtless welcome the opportunity to make a fool of the sheriff. Almost certainly there'd be powder burned. If blood was spilled...

Pearce, thoroughly disquieted, got up and began tramping the dark confines of his room. People could be such utter damn fools! What good would it do if he, Pearce, *did* go back? It might even turn out to make a bad matter worse. She had ordered him off the ranch. Be like waving a red rag in front of a bull.

The government wanted this country settled up; the politicians did, anyway, and were pulling all kinds of strings. The locators wanted the sodbusters' dollars. The farmers wanted the Indian lands and anything else they could get their plows into. The country was in a state of ferment, with nobody caring what might come of it as long as enough hard cash came their way. It was an age of greed, filled with ugliness and violence. Back East, the machines were cranking out Boss Tweeds, and people out here were grabbing everything in sight.

Until the railroad had decided to put Tolliver in back of a sheriff's star, the man had been nothing but a cow-town constable, an accepter of bribes and hush money, doing nothing but maintaining an illusion.

Fludd had been a hired gun.

Tara Drood herself had been scarcely of more consequence than the sorriest peon on her grandfather's ranch.

Now all this was changed. Each of these three had been unexpectedly thrust into positions of authority. Basic character had to be reckoned with, and a burgeoning pride that was unpredictable. The circuit judge was gone, but the court order the man had handed down could be the spark that would explode the powder keg.

Filled with dark thoughts, Pearce retrieved the pinched-out stogie from his coat and rekindled it, worried, trying to reach some decision he could feel was morally right.

Should he ride with the posse if Tolliver went back? Should he see the Indian Agent? Try to persuade Harry Chalkchild to give Star Circle more time?

None of these things could hold out much promise if Tolliver took the bit in his teeth. Further talk with Tara offered nothing at all, yet he was impelled to go back, to try one more time. He remembered her as she had looked that first night across the hall in her patchwork of castoffs, frightened but defiant, before Ames' door. There'd been something enormously appealing about her.

He tried to pin down what he felt, that elusive something which had quickened his pulses. Surely it was more than a mere animal magnetism, the attraction youth held for a man who was getting older ... He could still feel the power of it surging through him, see her expression, the bittersweet mouth with the provocative red lips too wide for her face, the eyes too knowing. Was it the eyes or the mouth that kept reaching out for him?

He had sensed the dark gleaming wildness back of her challenging stare, the fire of a womanliness that could spell heaven on earth for the man who could reach the trust that was in her. For that man there would be no more groping or stumbling, no more far trails beckoning. She'd be the alpha and the omega. He could see again her breasts lifting to the turmoil inside her, and outrage tightened all the lines of his face when he remembered that tinhorn she had tied herself up to.

*　　*　　*

Tolliver, when he got back to town, stomped into his office in a lather of fury. The only good part of the whole sorry business was the

143

knowledge that nobody had been there to see it. To be run off by a chit of a rattlebrained girl!

He swore at the sloe-eyed Indian faces sullenly observing him from the stench of barred cells. He shook the jailer awake, handed a shotgun to the man and sent him out to make the rounds. He paced the floor, occasionally cursing as the spleen boiled inside him. By God, he'd make her sorry! Past grievances crowded his mind and he swore in black anger. Treat him like dirt, would she!

He stormed out on the street in another spate of swearing. It was time these damn cow barons got a dose of their own!

*　　　*　　　*

The sun was two hours high when Tara, awakening in the canopied bed, thrust slim legs over the side and with bare feet found the floor. She sat a moment, knuckling the sleep from her eyes, recalling Tig Tolliver's precipitate departure. The face of the preacher came into her mind, crowding out everything else, and she got irritably up and slipped into her clothes.

She started for the kitchen, only to stop part way down the hall to wonder why she had overslept and what it was that had awakened her. A feeling of urgency took her into the front room. There were sounds outside, the stamp and whickering of horses, a muted grumble of voices.

She ran to a window, but nothing moved in her range of vision. Frowning, filled with an unaccountable alarm, she threw up the sash and put her head out. Beyond the day pen she saw the Star Circle riders, back from Twin Peaks! But what were they sitting their horses out there for? She went outside, filled with a gnawing disquiet, and ran toward them, seeing the queer way they bunched together, motionless.

She came up to them a little breathless, but only Fludd would meet her glance.

'Didn't you move them?'

'Sure, we moved them,' Fludd said, giving her back stare for stare.

Her look flashed across the others, finding nothing to relax the building tension. She saw their locked faces, inscrutable as rock. There was a surliness here, an undefined reluctance about them as though, in some unexplainable way, she was herself responsible for the strangeness she sensed in them.

Her glance whipped back to the man she'd made range boss.

'There's been a little mistake,' Fludd said, flapping the reins against his boot. His eyes considered her, bold almost to insolence. 'We seen this jasper duckin' round as we come up. Seemed like he might of had notions about them horses, way he was acting. Looking to be tryin' to Injun up on 'em. I yelled. He run. I yanked my gun an' let 'im have it.'

She followed his eyes toward the nearest enclosure. Suddenly, frozen, she saw between poles the crumpled shape sprawled half in and half out, a pearl-gray gaiter incongruously protruding below one hiked-up pantsleg.

Everything round her started to whirl. She caught at her throat.

'Too bad,' Fludd said. 'Course, it ain't like we couldn't git along without him, but why didn't the damn fool stop when I hollered? How was I to know?'

She wouldn't let herself faint, but she was cold deep inside, her legs feeling brittle as pipestems. She thought of Jesusita with her arms hugged about her. *You will never get anything from a cat but its hide.*

She wouldn't even get that. A terrible numbness seemed to have hold of her. At any moment she might lose her balance or be snatched by the wind that was roaring up out of the darkness.

How was I to know?

That was what he'd said.

Wrenching her stare from Ames' body, she found Fludd's face. He had known, all right. The whole story was there in the twist of his lips, in the cut of his eyes.

He grinned, not trying to hide it.

The cold crept all through her. Yet the skin of her body, the whole shivering length of her, seemed enveloped in flame.

146

Turning, she stumbled off toward the house.

CHAPTER TWENTY

When Pearce got up and went down to breakfast, the hungover stuff of unpalatable dreams still tramped through his thoughts with all the portent of disaster. The whole time he was eating he kept thinking of the facets of his relationship to Tara, frowning and bedeviled with convictions he couldn't escape. With the food gone, he still sat there, lost in the bogs of the conclusions he'd come onto.

It was ridiculous to assume that people never changed; they were changing all the while they moved from cradle to the grave. The proof was in their faces. Even their notions were subject to change. Nothing remained static. Change was the very basis of life, so why should he think Tara Drood was above this common denominator? Even Old Mike, who'd been rough as a cob, had mellowed to the extent of tolerating squatters, the LeGrues and those others up around Twin Peaks. Was Tara more adamant, more stubborn, than Mike?

It was Tara's youth and inexperience that made her seem so contentious and heartless. Youth was the age of rebellion, a time of impatience, of scorn for established usage. Youth had to be shown, and when she saw her mistakes...

Deep in his throat, Pearce growled with pity. There was no way he could get through to her. She would have to find out for herself, but by the time she woke up it could be too late. Nothing could save Star Circle; nothing she might do was going to hold the ranch together. Stubbornness and pride—the bitter bones of her ambition—would take her headlong into heartbreak.

Pearce threw down his napkin and quit the hotel. He got his horse from one of the liveries and rode to the house of the Indian Agent. The man scowled but listened, afterward shaking his head.

'That may very well be true, but it doesn't excuse her. Along with the ranch she inherited Mike's obligations. She has made no effort to meet them. You tell me she'll pay. I can't believe it. She's Mike all over, more uncaring than he was. A case in point is what happened to Meyers. Jock Meyers came into this country with Mike. When he wouldn't put up with her craziness, what did she do? Offered that gun fighter Mike's job to get rid of him. She threw all those Mexicans off Star Circle, her own mother's people!'

He considered Pearce grimly. 'I don't question your sincerity, Parson, but I'm faced with obligations myself. I have to look out for these wards of the government. Star Circle's taken over more than ninety thousand acres of

148

Indian lands. Two years they have held it without paying these people one thin dime. This is fact. Chalkchild went out there—'

'Did he talk with Tara?'

'She's responsible. That girl is Star Circle. So we went to the law. The sheriff rode out there with an order from the court. *He* saw her. She ran him off with a rifle!'

Pearce said quietly, 'What will you do?'

The man scowled. 'I don't know. I suppose it will depend on the sheriff. He's gone back. The court's ruling gives us the right to impound cattle to satisfy the debt.' He looked at Pearce thoughtfully. 'That's one side of the coin.'

'What's the other?'

'A large number of her cows are on Indian grass.'

Pearce thought, *She'll never give them up.*

'If the sheriff can't function, I have one move left,' the Agent said. 'I can go to the fort and invoke Federal aid.' He looked at Pearce darkly. 'I expect that's what I will have to do, probably. I don't think anything short of troops will make these pirates toe the line.'

*　　*　　*

It was high noon when the sound of hoofs pulled Tara to the window to find a cavalcade of riders converging on the yard. The men were heavily armed; in addition to six-shooters, a number of the horsebackers were flourishing

149

antiquated muskets and buffalo guns, and the scowling look on their faces made it readily apparent this mob was not out here to exercise their horses.

She saw the black bristling mustache and badge of Tig Tolliver, but before she could reach and throw open the door the flat challenge of Fludd's voice rang out. 'That's far enough!' he called harshly.

Tara ran breathlessly onto the gallery. 'Wait!'

Fludd's gaunt shape held the middle of the yard. He stood, legs braced, chest and jaw shoved forward, right hand spread above the butt of his pistol. His eyes were bright with recklessness and scorn. Back of him the sun caught the wink of Winchester barrels.

He said, without ever looking at the girl, 'What kind of a rusty you tryin' to pull, Tolliver, bargin' in here with a mob like that?'

'This here's a posse,' the sheriff blustered. 'We're here with an order from the court. Now throw down them guns—'

'Like hell!' Fludd sneered. 'You want them guns, let's see you take 'em!'

'Wait—' Tara cried again, running into the yard. She stopped midway between the sheriff and Fludd. 'What kind of an order?' she said, facing Tolliver.

Tig, licking his lips, dug a hand into his coat and fetched out a paper while the assortment of barflies and squatters behind him looked to be wishing themselves someplace else. 'Got it right here,' the sheriff said, battling the wind to get it unfolded. He peered nervously at Fludd, then kneed his horse forward, leaning down to thrust it out to the girl.

'Don't touch it!' Fludd yelled.

Tara took the paper and read it with a shoulder hunched against the wind. Some of the words she'd never seen before, and the gist of the thing was so obscured in the clutter of legal terminology she found the heart of the matter hard to get hold of.

'That's a injunction,' Tolliver hastened to explain, 'a kind of restrainer, I guess you might call it. Means the Court has ruled you can't move no cattle till Star Circle's indebtedness to them Injuns is satisfied.' He said, with an edge to his grin, 'Now you know. You been served right an' proper.'

Tara, smiling up at him, tore the paper across and tore it again, flinging the pieces into the wind. 'You'll have to talk louder. I can't seem to make out a thing you been saying.'

Tolliver snarled. 'It'll come to you, you try movin' them cattle. You're like to turn up inside of a jail! You goddam Droods—'

A gun sharply spoke. The sheriff's hat jumped. 'Get goin',' Fludd said, 'before I cut you loose of them britches. And take them friggin' weedbenders with you.'

Those were pretty stiff words. Some of the posse looked as if they were fixing to get

151

themselves put on record. But nothing came of it; they were more afraid of Fludd than they were about what might later be said of them. Nobody hankered to be a dead hero.

It could have ended right there, but Tolliver had more to live down than the rest of them. Injured pride and bitterness drove a hand at his hip.

He had the barrel of his six-shooter half out of leather when the first bullet hit him, smashing him like a fist against the cantle. 'No!' Tara shouted, whirling with frightened eyes to peer at Fludd.

Fludd showed his teeth in a crack of hard grin. Through the whistle and lash of pummeling wind came a wild beat of hoofs. Flame and smoke jumped again from the snout of Fludd's pistol. All over the yard guns were flashing and pounding in a stench of black powder. The girl's voice was lost. In the hammering din the posse came apart. Crazed horses, unmanageable, running blind in their terror, broke and fled in a dozen directions.

The whole action was over in scarcely more than half a minute. One riderless horse ran limping, reins flapping, after the routed Law. One twisted shape lay like a bundle of dropped clothes ten feet from Tara.

With the toe of his boot Fludd rolled the man over. Not Tolliver. 'Some poor slob,' the range boss said, 'that come out here fer a belly laugh.'

As in a trance Tara stared at the face of Joe Wheeler, bleakly remembering the red dress she'd worn the night Ames had knocked him down in the hotel dining room at More Oaks.

Now they were both dead.

The bones in her legs seemed to have turned to water. Fludd's stare burned into her, and she pulled up her head, frightened, wondering with a sick dismay what she'd let herself in for, where it would all end.

Stepping close, Fludd slapped her, then slapped her again. She stumbled back, tears stinging her eyes. The yard and buildings, Fludd's scowl, swam into focus, and he stepped back. 'That's better. We done what we had to.'

'You didn't have to *kill* him!'

'That's where you're wrong. That crowd's been showed. They'll be a long time gittin' up nerve to come back—'

'Is killing,' she asked on a shuddery breath, 'your answer to everything?'

'Gits the job done, don't it?' Fludd looked at her toughly. 'You got no call to be jumpin' at me—you think anybody'll foller Tolliver again?' He laughed harshly, the bold slanch of his stare hotly touching her breasts and hips. 'Git it through your head. You're into this now too deep to back out. You're goddam lucky to hev a man like me around!'

*　　*　　*

153

Thoroughly understanding, Tara bit her lip, feeling panic like an icy ball against the walls of her stomach. There was no place she could run. There was a roaring in her ears like surf caroming off a rocky shore; she could feel it rushing over her in a blinding dazzle of swirling light, and she fought bitterly against her fear.

Somewhere leather screaked. Boots tramped across a brittle silence. A hand took firm hold of her elbow, and Fludd's rusty cheeks swam back into focus. A voice just behind and to the right of her said, 'I think you've had about enough of this for now.'

Her whole body loosened. She'd have fallen if he hadn't kept hold of her. She began to shake uncontrollably. 'Pearce!' she whispered. 'Take me to the house.'

She didn't see the ugliness in Fludd's dark face, the spasmodic twitching of his hands, or the terrible way he stood glaring after them. She knew only the strong, blessed feel of Pearce's arms, bearing her up and carrying her away, the rugged, comforting beat of his heart as she snuggled against it too spent to think, burrowing her face into the haven of his shoulder.

CHAPTER TWENTY-ONE

All was dark when Tara opened her eyes. She did not, right at first, care a thing about time or even wonder where she was, being content just to lie there, dimly aware of being filled with a strange and wonderful tranquillity. If this was what being married was like ... She pushed out an arm, came up onto her elbow, a sense of loss traveling through her, an increasing apprehension. Fully awake, she came bolt upright, remembering Ames between the poles of the pen, the flat opaqueness of Wheeler's dead stare.

It all came back. She sprang up, peering wildly.

Pearce! Where was Pearce?

She recalled now ordering him off the ranch. But he'd come back ... hadn't he? Was it only a dream?

The floor was ice against her feet. She searched for her slippers—things she hadn't known until in More Oakes Ames had fetched these for her ... Ames who was dead between the poles of that pen.

She shivered, pulled on a robe—another reminder of Ames. Why was everything so still? Where *was* everyone? Had Fludd gone? Had he taken the crew?

She pulled open the door. Breath held, she

stepped into the cavernous murk of the hall. It was colder out here, the chill feel of it dragging at the folds of her robe, curling around her like water. And black!

Tolliver's posse reeled through her thoughts just the way it had come apart under the guns. The sheriff rode past with mouth widely stretched, the bloody front of him twisting, legs clinging desperately to the horse, trying to stay in the saddle as the terrified animal broke in fright. And Fludd, toughly grinning, wreathed in the red gouts of flame from his pistol.

You're into this now too deep to back out.

Her skin burned in the grip of the man's bold stare. Was it all just a dream, like the feel of Pearce's arms? Where was her mother?

A slash of light lay under the kitchen door like a knife. She stopped, her breath locked inside her. But Fludd, if he came, wouldn't move into the kitchen.

Teeth clenched, she pulled the door open.

She saw nothing but Pearce. His presence nearly unnerved her. The room started to spin. She went stumbling toward him across the heaving floor. Strong hands, immeasurably comforting, took hold of and guided her, steering her into a chair. She felt cheated when their grip dropped away. 'They've gone to Stroud,' Pearce explained, when she stared at him blankly.

'Fludd,' he said, 'and your Star Circle hands. Had to get the excitement of it off their chests.'

Tara said with open scorn, 'I don't see anything so much to stampeding a mess of hoe slingers!'

'More to it than that.' Pearce sighed. 'What it amounts to is, they've stood off the Law.' He considered her gravely. 'Did you get a little rest?'

He was sharper than she'd figured. She was going to have to use more care, revealing only those things she had a need for him to see. 'So you're sure-enough here.' She studied the dark face of him. 'I thought for a time I must have dreamed it. Fludd truly did chase that posse away?'

Pearce nodded. She found the taciturn planes of his cheeks inscrutable. His glance withstood her probing, yet . . . he must have felt something. Why else had he returned?

She didn't try to understand how his being here could so incalculably have changed the whole slant of her thinking. That he was here was the big thing. All she had to find now was how to make the most of it. She'd have to be careful. He was easily shocked.

She looked up. 'What do you figure I'd better do?'

Sensing his approval she was secretly amused. But her satisfaction disappeared when he said: 'Get rid of Fludd. Put away these ridiculous notions, that wicked pride which hides the truth, and be the woman, walking humbly, God in his His mercy intended you to

157

be. Pay off those wretched Indians—'

'But I can't!' she cried. 'I don't have the money!'

'You've got Mike's cattle.'

'But they're practically worthless! At the price of beef now—'

'They belong to Mike's creditors.'

'And what about *me*!' She spun away from him, furious, unable to hide the wild climb of her anger.

'You've got no alternative,' Pearce said quietly. 'Give them the cattle, get off the Reservation—'

'You must think I'm *loco*!'

It made no difference now that originally she'd intended to pay off those savages with cattle—all that was changed with the loss of Ames and his St Louis packing house. All she had now was Mike's cows and the land that was hers only as long as she could keep it. What Pearce asked was impossible. Without money, with no real title to this broad sea of grass, she *had* to keep the cattle. All her gun-hung riders were not enough without them. She had to show justification, a bona fide use...

Pearce said: 'It's vanity that blinds you, this foolish pride you set such store by. The treasures of the world are as perishable as paper. Have you forgotten what Christ said to the Tempter?' He held her with the stab of his eyes. 'Man cannot live by grass alone.'

'We've got to be practical—'

'The word is a snare, an invention of the Devil. Believe me, Tara'—his voice shook with earnestness—'you cannot keep either the cattle or the land. You've got to realize this.'

She was shaken. He could see it.

'Look at it straight. Give yourself a chance.'

She scrubbed a hand across her eyes.

The glow of his face showed the depth of his compassion. She was almost persuaded.

'But Joe Wheeler—'

'The man's been buried.' Pearce bent over and picked his hat off the floor.

Tara, biting her lip, said, 'What will they do—the town crowd, I mean?'

'I don't expect they'll do much of anything. Grumble some, maybe.'

This was what she wanted to hear, that you could thumb your nose at the Law with impunity. She drew a deep breath. All she really had to worry about was Fludd. But she had to be sure. 'You mean the Law—'

'The Law,' Pearce said, 'in a country like this is the men who are hired to uphold it, in this case Tolliver. Times will change—they're changing now. Any law, to be workable, must have the community—the whole weight of it, behind it. To get this support there's got to be respect. People like Mike never gave it a chance.'

He looked straight at her. 'Fludd finished Tolliver. That's one of the reasons you've got to get rid of him. Because of him, and because

159

you're Mike's kin, you're suspect. You've got to show people you're not cut from the same cloth. But that's only part of it.' He cuffed the dust from his hat. 'You can't expect to wipe out what's happened or separate anyone from the things they believe without going the whole way. You got to make a clean sweep, get rid of everything the old man left. You'll probably still be suspect, but in your own mind at least—'

'I can live with my mind!'

'Then what are you twistin' your eyes away for? The day of the big spread is gone. Like the buffalo. This ground will support twenty times—'

'You can't grow crops without water! Where'll they get it?'

'You'll have to pipe it from the river,' Pearce said, as if he were handing it straight down from Moses. 'You can't impose your will on this people. You can't stand off Chalkchild—the thing is out of his hands. The tribe is turning ugly. It's the Agent's job to look out for them, and he won't have a job if they dig up their hatchets. Look at it, girl ... There'll be blood on the bushes an' burned-out ranches. The Government will move them and throw open these lands.' He shook his head at her. 'Where will Star Circle be?'

She watched sullenly, the whole look of her rebellious. It wasn't so much that she was questioning what he said—how *could* she

160

disbelieve it with every sign and signal-smoke towering black in front of her? No, it was the innate stubbornness, the damned Drood pride in her.

He could see her pride spreading like a noxious vine, clutching, strangling his words, bringing her inexorably nearer the pit of eternal damnation.

She put out a hand, going back half a step before the threat of the man's enormous earnestness. Uneasy and confused, wandering in the maze of her uncertainty, nothing seemed as she had seen it. But if she did what Pearce wanted ... She could not abide the dreary vision of herself without the backdrop of this sprawling grass empire Mike had torn from the West. Without Star Circle—why, she'd be nothing! If he thought anything at all of her...

'The blood,' Pearce was saying, 'can you stand the awful stench of it?'

Glaring, she clapped both hands against her ears, hating, despising, yet more than a little afraid of his strength, his hectoring persistence that wanted to confound and make a fool of her.

Why should she give up what was hers?

She spun away from him in resentment and, outraged, stalked the length of the room. Why should she care what he thought? Fludd would take care of her—he'd look out for her interests; his gun would chase the coyotes away. Let them howl. What did *she* care!

But, strangely, she did. She tried to laugh such foolishness out of her head, but Fludd's stare confronted her—bold, contemptuously possessive. The dark blood whipped into her cheeks. She could never control him: she knew this instinctively. Any alliance with Fludd would be surrender. And where would Star Circle be then?

Tara shivered. She looked back at Pearce.

She could feel the strength in him. It was more than muscle—something you couldn't pin down or explain, a solidness as of rock, a reaching out, a comforting. He was like a towering mountain. Something to be thrust between herself and Fludd.

She came wholly around. 'Have you—Have you seen my husband?'

He shook his head.

'I suppose,' she said, 'we'd better bury him,' and saw the shock of it explode through Pearce. Like cracks shooting out from a hole in a window—that plain.

'Fludd?' Pearce said.

Even his voice seemed queer, quiet, as controlled as everything about him was, but strangely hoarse, a wildness churning up out of its depths that was frightening and, inexplicably—to Tara—deliciously exciting.

She watched him, fascinated. 'I suppose Ames was trying to get a horse from the corral ... He'd been busting to go to town. Fludd was just riding in. He whipped out a gun. Ames' back was turned.' She got a lantern out of the chimney corner. 'The whole crew saw it.'

'You're sure he's dead?'

She lifted the globe and put a match to the wick. He was dead, all right. She put a hand to her breast. 'I don't know,' she said, 'but he looked awful like it. He wasn't doing any talking.'

Pearce took the lantern, and Tara followed him out.

'Which way?'

'Off there.' Lamps made bright squares of the bunkhouse windows. She could feel Pearce's eyes. 'That one, just this side of the day pen.'

Pearce strode off with the lantern. She almost had to run to keep up with him. A door opened someplace and light shafted over the shale hubbly ground. She caught the mutter of voices. As Pearce lifted the lantern, she saw the scuffed earth.

'This wasn't a dream, was it?'

'He was right there,' she said. 'Folded over those rails.'

'Playing possum, probably.'

'He was dead,' she said flatly.

Boots moved into the lantern's brightness, and belted shells made a brassy shine as Fludd stepped scowling out of the shadows. 'You lookin' fer somethin'?'

'Ames,' Pearce said.

Fludd's breathing grew louder. A slow wind

ruffled the man's roan hair. 'Hmm—too bad about him. But it could happen to anyone rammin' aroun' this place after dark.'

'It wasn't dark!' Tara cried.

'Well, it's dark enough now.' Fludd's glance swung to Pearce, and the hunched points of his shoulders, shifting, sent a hand swiveling back to hover above the bone butt of his pistol. 'Wouldn't be no trouble to put you away, too.'

CHAPTER TWENTY-TWO

Pearce, in the confusions of the days that followed, began to wonder if a man ever had the faintest notion of what actually went on inside the head of a woman. He had thought he had Tara Drood figured out; he had been sure of it after that go-round with Fludd when, back at the house, plainly frightened and apparently penitent, in a wild burst of tears she had begged him to stay.

He had supposed she meant till she could get rid of Fludd, but it certainly hadn't worked out that way. So far as he could see, she'd made no attempt to cut the ranch loose of him. Every time Pearce brought Fludd into their talk, she'd look scared or jump up mad and go stalking off.

Several times, completely disgusted, Pearce had been about to climb his horse and clear out, and twice he'd even got as far as the corrals. The first of these occasions had been the middle of a morning three days after the rout of the More Oaks posse. A cold driving wind off the frozen slopes had the whole crew hugging the pot-bellied stoves when a blue-cheeked hombre on a near foundered horse, pounding over the planks of the bridge, stumbled into the yard through a gray fall of flakes.

Fludd, getting into his sheepskin, appeared. His shout, slamming into the wind a moment later, pulled all hands to the windows. 'Come outa there!' he bellowed, inter-larding the words with a crackle of language better suited to a drovers' convention than to the ears of the girl who stood taking it in.

Pearce stepped out. Tara, pulling on a coat, hurried after him over the crunchy boards of the frost-coated gallery. She was just in time to see the crew, every man with a rifle, set off for the horse trap. 'I'll handle it,' she called, running to intercept the still-swearing range boss, who was just wheeling away from the courier's cringing shape.

The man was a jackleg Mormon who ran a few cows over north of the mountain. Nothing but the hope of currying favor could have fetched him here in this kind of weather. Pearce said, coming up to him, 'Better tend to that horse and get in out of the cold. What's all the excitement?'

'Squatters!'

Pearce continued to stare.

'A hell's smear of that crowd the railroad's sucked in is on the east fringe of this spread, diggin' in—must be close on t' half a hundred of 'em! All up an' down them fine creek medders, them ones we was hayin' las' fall fer Ol' Mike.'

'Better come inside, Tobie,' Tara said, moving into their talk. The white plume of her breath was whipped away. 'Put your nag in the barn. While you're rubbin' him down, I'll see if I can't scare up a little whisky.'

Mumbling his thanks the old man tramped off, the tired horse plodding patiently after him. Tara still stood beside Pearce, shivering. 'Well,' she said, with nervous impatience, 'I can't think what we're standin' around here for!'

'Fludd's going after those people, isn't he?'

'He's goin' to take a look.'

'I suppose he's just lugging those rifles to lean on!'

Tara said sullenly, 'He'll do what he has to.' She started for the house.

'He doesn't have to do anything.'

'Go ahead an' tell him!'

Pearce swung around. 'I will.'

She caught his arm. 'Don't be a damn fool!'

Cold eyes peered through the driving snow. 'We might as well all be a pack of fools together—'

'He'll kill you, Pearce!'

'Am I more important than those women an' kids?'

Her eyes wouldn't meet the blaze of his stare. She kept hold of him, though. She said fiercely, 'Stay out of this.' Her teeth began to chatter. 'There won't be trouble—he told me there wouldn't.'

'And you let me believe you were going to break with him!'

'I am—of *course* I am!' She grabbed his arm tighter against her. 'I wouldn't lie to you, Pearce.' Hazel eyes looked widely into his own. 'You know that, don't you?'

The warmth of her grip, the twisting female feel of the woman burned through him like fire. Pearce tried to fight it, but the hunger was in him.

She said: 'It's just a test. Fludd will call their bluff, mebbe burn a few things ... All he wants is to throw a scare into them.' She rushed on, the landslide tumble of her words surrounding him. 'You said yourself I should give the grass away. That's what I'm aimin' at—but, Pearce, I can't just plain let them *steal* it!'

Of course she couldn't. If there had got to be stealing, the Droods had first rights. And she had cows on that range. Cows were cash money—not much, maybe, right now, but a sight more than you could get for a nester.

He felt discouraged; he couldn't seem to come onto any firm ground. The wild skirl of the snow and the moaning wind made a curtain past which he could scarcely see.

'I've told him no one's to be hurt,' she said again.

Pearce let her pull him along toward the house.

* * *

That was bad enough to be remembering, but the second deal was worse. It was so terribly final, and it was done in broad daylight, with no excuses offered.

It was the fourth day after Fludd took off to chase squatters.

Not all of the crew had come back with the boss, but those that had, taking advantage of the snow melt, had put off their coats and were lolling around in front of the buildings, chewing or smoking while they soaked up the sun.

Be colder out there on the back of a horse, but nobody was fixing to ride till they had to. If any of them missed Jock Meyers, it wasn't evident. Instead of climbing out in the middle of the night, under the new dispensation the Star Circle crew seldom hauled up its galluses short of eight o'clock, and mighty little was said if a fellow took longer.

On this particular occasion they'd tumbled out later than usual, tied on the feedbags like bankers, and had been fooling around pretty near the whole morning waiting on Fludd to lay out the day's jobs, when this derby-hatted jasper, bundled to the gills, came in off the stage road forking, of all things, a freckled gray mare.

No self-respecting ranny would have been caught dead on the back of a mare. Comment rose like a covey of quail as they watched him travel the ruts of the lane.

'Corset drummer.'

'Gold-brick salesman.'

'Sheepman,' the cook said. 'Smell 'em fur as you kin see one.'

'Remittance man.'

'Lookit them yaller shoes! A Boston. One of them Simon-pure kind! Fishcakes fer breakfast ever' Sunday mornin'.'

'That goddam chump's a preacher. Come out here after Pearce, I reckon.'

'Nope,' said the wrangler, putting aside the headstall he was pleating, 'that there hombre is one of them pitcher takers.'

Fludd, coming out of the foreman's shack, walked over and squatted down by straw boss Birch. 'Green as paint,' Birch said with a snort.

Fludd said, squinting, 'Might be one of them railroad snoopers.'

The mare clopped over the rattle of planks. Fludd's cheeks pulled tighter as she came into the yard.

'Howdy,' the man said, peering around. 'This the Star Circle?'

He sat the mare like he was glued to her. He had little pop eyes, and about a third of his windburned face was taken up with a mustache, coarse and wiry as a field full of stubble.

'We don't want any,' Birch said, scowling up at him.

The stranger laughed. But the laugh, Fludd noticed, never got up past his mouth. 'Getting warm,' the man said, pulling open his coat. 'Mind if I get down?' His glance cut over to Fludd.

'What's your business?' Birch said.

'Thought you might have some cattle you'd be glad to get rid of.'

Fludd got up off his heels, crease-lidded. 'You never come out here to buy no cattle.'

In the congealing quiet, Pearce, on the gallery, could hear every word. 'That's right,' the man said. 'You the ridin' boss here?'

'You ain't been travelin' all night to ask for no job.'

'Nope. I'm lookin' for Fludd.'

'You're lookin' right at him.'

Tara came out of the house. She had on her town clothes and was getting into a pair of gauntlets. Frowning, she stepped into the yard. 'What's he want?' she called.

No one bothered to answer. Not one pair of eyes left the two men's faces. It was as though some compulsion stronger than themselves held them bound in their tracks, incapable of movement.

'It figures,' the man said, and put a hand on his pistol.

Fludd's eyes gleamed. Pearce sensed what was coming, but he didn't act fast enough. While he was quitting the gallery, the man on the horse said: 'I want you, Fludd. We got a bunch of dead settlers—'

No one saw Fludd draw. One moment his hand was empty. The next, while everyone else stood frozen and Pearce himself paused in midstride, the mustached stranger, far back in his saddle, slipped to the side and then, through the crash of Fludd's gun, toppled to the ground.

Tara stood rooted.

Fludd's ugly eyes raked Pearce's face. In all the crew there wasn't one released breath. Then Birch shifted his chew with solemn care. He wiped the palms of his hands on the hips of his Levi's, chunked a quick look at Fludd, and stepped stiffly across to go down by the man. Grunting, he pulled him over.

Birch got up, dusting his hands off.

They could all see the badge on the dead man's shirt.

Fludd had killed a federal marshal.

CHAPTER TWENTY-THREE

Tara stiffly turned and without a word went into the house, the sound of the door thinly sharp in that quiet. Pearce rammed his fists deep into his pockets. If there had been any doubt in his mind it was gone. Star Circle was dead. It had been killed just as sure by Fludd's gun as this marshal.

Pearce looked at the man, at the gaunt, bony length of him hunched so narrow eyed over that pistol. Seen in the cold statistics of his actions there were some, Pearce supposed, who must consider him a monster, a cold-blooded killer—and he was that, of course. But there were other facets to him.

No man was entirely bad; humans were human, and even the best revealed room for improvement, though it was hard sometimes to remember this. As for the worst, well, a man ought to be seen in the light of his environment. Guns were Fludd's business. Come right down to it, he was not greatly different from Old Man Mike, John Chisum, or others of that stripe; more direct, perhaps, but scarcely more ruthless. It was a ruthless age.

Fludd, lifting the weapon, blew the smoke from its barrel, his heavy-lidded stare never leaving Pearce's face. 'Somethin' on your mind?'

No amount of talk could sponge off the slate or put the marshal back into his saddle. He turned away, shaking his head, and went into the house.

What good was preaching? The people who needed it most never listened ... well, hardly ever, anyway. Pearce irritably knew there was more to it than that. But he was human, too. In his present frame of mind he couldn't see much hope for anyone. He told himself, however, he had better find a little. He thought of other ranches where lawmen had been killed, and could not remember one that had survived any great while after.

The ranch wasn't his concern. His job was to save people. To steer them away from their follies and at least *try* to look out for their souls. But he was only one man.

He glared down at clenched fists, wanting to hit walls that were forever in front of him. They'd be needing him in town. He ought to be out there now with those Apaches, talking some sense into that riled chief. He ought to be with the Agent, with the bereaved among the homesteader crowd; there were countless needs crying out for his attentions, all of them worthy, many of them urgent ... And here he was, tied to Star Circle, grinding his teeth like a frustrated child!

He could bolster his stand with any number of good reasons, find answers in plenty—time and distance, to name just a couple. Someone's

173

hand had to be on the pulse. The heart of this whole devil's brew was Star Circle.

But the real truth was Tara.

Nothing wrong with that. She was part of his flock, her own worst enemy, a girl who had to be saved from herself. He strode around through the furnishings, seeing but not noticing, barely aware that he was on his feet at all.

Why should he be in such a turmoil? Was he so determined he was right? Was he loath to examine his motives more closely? Was his zeal wholly real, this desire to save lives? Was there more to this than pastoral duty?

Of course not! What else could there be? He shunted these thoughts uncomfortably aside, but an elusive unrest he found mightily disturbing continued to gnaw at him. He ought, he thought, to get the girl away. He kept turning it over, reluctant to face her.

The cook banged a kettle, but Pearce wasn't hungry. Tara's urchin features, in a hundred different guises, continued to float in the foreground of every problem. Ames had come here figuring to take over. Meyers' trouble, though different, might have sprung from the same disease. Fludd had knocked over both of them. Was it reasonable to assume he, Pearce, was immune? With Fludd, Pearce suspected, loyalty was something to be farmed out—like his gun and the fear its efficiency commanded.

This place was bad for Tara. Too much was

remindful of so many things it was better for her to forget. The violent present, the hateful past, the bitter cling of unhealed hurts—

Pearce turned, breath caught, hard listening. In this magnified quiet he was half convinced the scream had been imagined. When it came again, it had a strangled sound, too faint to have crossed the windy yard. It was here someplace inside these walls. *Her* voice!

Down the hall he dashed, trying doors, flinging them wide. He was like a man bereft of his senses, heedless of peril.

This might be a trap, and for a split second he wondered, but he was too concerned to pause. Those screams had been triggered by terror, and terror's cold touch had hold of him, too. He found himself, panting, before the closed door of the kitchen.

He flung himself at it behind a hunched shoulder, knowing only he had to get in there quick. Something broke. The door yawed and half fell, drunkenly canted.

Pearce, clutching the jamb, saw the old woman in a tangle of petticoats, crumped and bloody by the overturned table. The rake of his stare found Tara, eyes enormous above the ripped dress, flat against the far wall.

And then he found Fludd.

*   *   *

Pearce thought he would never get his eyes

open. When he did, he wished he hadn't. He tried again, owlishly blinking in the glare of a lamp at a room dizzily spinning with the blue shapes of men. He tried to beat off the hampering arms. The scene heaved and buckled. 'He's comin' round,' someone said, and Pearce thought his skull must be split wide open. Giddy blackness closed in. He felt the floor rushing up at him.

Next thing he could be sure of was the raw burn of whisky. He struck out, coughing and spluttering, trying to break through, whaling blindly into the solid barrier of a wall. The shock snapped his eyes open. That whisky must have put new strength in him. He clung to the wall, breathing hard, coming out of it.

He recognized the Star Circle kitchen. The blue crowding of shapes became dusty troopers, yellow-legged horse soldiers. 'He's a black Irisher, Parson ... hit 'im again!' Laughter came out of the one holding the lamp; the red face in front of him belonged to a sergeant. That blanket-covered mound on the floor would be Tara's mother; he remembered now the pitiable draggle of skirts. It all came back ... the girl's scared eyes ... the wickedness of Fludd's grin, the flame gouting from his pistol.

Pearce felt his head, visibly cringing, unable to hold back his groans. He had tried, he thought bitterly—God, how he'd tried! flinging himself across the give of that door. He

176

just hadn't been man enough. Not against Fludd.

' ... musta left you fer dead,' the sergeant was saying. 'Sure as hell looked it, with that blood all over—'

'The girl!' Pearce cried, shaking him. '*Where is she?*'

'Girl?' The red face looked stupid. 'Oh!' A great light broke. 'You mean Mrs Ames.' He shook his head. 'Ain't nobody seen 'er. Wasn't no one here when we came but you an''—he looked toward the blanket—'the ol' lady there.'

A harsh scrape of shovels came in from outside. A faint embarrassment touched the sergeant, and he said with a leavening of pity: 'You better set down, Padre. We're liable to be here—'

'She's got to be found!'

Eyes regarding him quizzically, the florid face nodded. 'Sure an' that's what the major says. But 'tis black as the Divil's hip pocket out there.' The man held up his lamp a little, peering, plainly dubious. 'If you kin make it up to the front, I expect the major'll be wantin' to swap a few words.'

Pearce, looking somewhat dubious himself, ran the heel of a hand across the rasp of his jaw. 'All right,' he growled finally, and tramped after the man, the others falling back to let them into the hall.

The major, in the living room, was with a

pair of captains. There was a sharp click of heels. 'Sargint McIlvey, sor, reportin' with the casualty.'

'Good Lord, Pearce!' the major cried, stepping forward. 'I hadn't realized—'

'Never mind,' Pearce said impatiently. 'What are you doing about finding Mrs Ames?'

'I can't find anyone until we get enough light to unravel their tracks. But I can tell you this,' the major said, bridling, 'she and that precious husband of hers are going to find out they can't thumb their noses at the U.S. Army!'

'I don't imagine,' Pearce replied, 'she'd even dream of such a thing.' He held up a hand as the officer started to interrupt. 'I'll admit it looks bad. I can understand your feelings. She's done some pretty foolish things—'

'She's done considerably more than that!'

'You could be mistaken,' Pearce said to the grim, scowling look of him. 'She's scarcely more than a child. Put yourself in her place. Inexperienced, marooned out here all her life, so desperate to get away she'd take up with a total stranger—'

'That's all very well,' the major said harshly, 'but facts are facts, and you can't get around them. All this killing, defaulting on her debts, illegal assumption of—'

'You'd be hard put to prove those charges, Major.'

The major looked at him, bristling. 'Do you deny most of this violence has come about

178

since Ames moved out here?'

'I hold no brief for Ames,' Pearce said. 'I suppose, if you're so minded, you could blame him for practically all of this trouble. Being dead, he's in no position to put up much of a holler.'

The major looked sharply at him. 'Are you telling me Ames is dead, Mr Pearce?'

'He's here, if you want to dig him up. And now, if you don't mind,' Pearce added, 'I think I'll sit down.' He sagged into a chair.

The major said at once, to one of the captains, 'Mr Stranch, fetch Mr Pearce some of that brandy.'

The shorter of the pair came over to Pearce with a bottle. 'You can go.' The major nodded to McIlvey. The sergeant, saluting, reluctantly departed. The other captain closed the hall door, and Pearce, with the fire of the brandy in his belly, showed more interest in what was happening. He met the major's somber regard.

The major said, 'I think, Mr Pearce, you've said too much to stop there. How did Ames die?'

'He was killed by that gunslinger, Fludd. Fludd claimed it was a mistake; says he thought Ames was a prowler. The girl tells a different story.'

'Perhaps you'd better let us have the whole thing. You married them. Start with that.'

So Pearce went over the facts as he knew them, starting at More Oaks the night he had found Tara Drood outside Ames' door. He gave them his impressions along with the rest of it, and when he had finished, the major shook his head.

He took a turn around the room, plainly uncomfortable. He came back, his harassed glance going over the faces of his officers. Stranch said, 'I suppose it could be like that.'

The other captain nodded. 'Seems a pretty good chance Fludd is figuring to take over.'

'It's preposterous,' the major said. 'What could he hope to gain? He can't stand off the whole U.S. Army!'

'He stood off the law,' Stranch reminded him dryly.

The major looked irascible. 'Of course,' he said, 'there's the matter of possession. In a time of change the man on the ground ...' He spread his hands in a shrug. 'It's a mess any way you look at it.'

'Supposing,' Pearce said, 'he aimed to marry Mrs Ames—'

'After killing her husband?'

'She stands alone,' Stranch said, 'if Pearce is right. If that's what he's after, he wouldn't have too much trouble. Any man who would shoot down a U.S. Marshal wouldn't let a woman's feelings stand between himself and an empire of grass.'

'And what about afterward?' the major asked testily. 'The man's no fool. He'd know that sooner or later—'

'A man like Fludd,' Pearce said, 'is hard to figure.' He put a hand gingerly up to his cloth-bound head. 'It's pretty obvious Mrs Ames intended to break up the ranch; you certainly can't think it has brought her any happiness.'

The major looked at him oddly. Stranch said: 'Perhaps we ought to try and catch some rest. We'll be up at first light...'

The major waved them away. Pearce said, after they had gone, 'Suppose, when we catch up with Fludd, he decides to make an all-out fight of it? I think we should consider what might happen to Mrs Ames.'

'She'll just have to take her chances, I guess.'

Pearce stared at him, scowling. 'That's a pretty hard thought.'

'I have my orders.' The major put a cigar into the clamp of white teeth. 'The ifs, ands, or buts of this have nothing to do with me.' He looked at Pearce blackly. 'If they're on the Reservation trying to gather up those cattle, I shall have to be governed by what happens after I've warned them.'

'The man will use Mrs Ames for a hostage, Major.'

'My orders are not concerned with individuals. If the cattle are moved in defiance of my warning, I shall have to consider it an act of rebellion. I'm sorry, Pearce. I have no alternative.'

*　　　*　　　*

181

Fludd, when he quit the yard at Star Circle, was about as riled as a man could get. Nothing was going the way he had planned it. It wasn't that the girl had put up a fight—that much he'd expected; but he had thought that when he cut Pearce down right in front of her she would be so crushed by her own impotence he would have no further trouble with her.

He had thought to come upon her alone in the kitchen, but Jesusita had been there. She'd come after him with a knife when he'd started for the girl, and he'd had to use his gun butt. Though he'd had to knock the girl around, she'd come after him like a wildcat when he'd put that slug through the preacher's head. They'd had to tie her into the saddle.

It hadn't set good with the men. Five of the bastards had slipped away and skinned out, leaving him short-handed. There wasn't a stinking one he dared trust. Looking around at their sullen faces, he cursed them, knowing they'd quit him first chance they got.

The girl rode in stubborn silence, never opening her mouth no matter what he said to her. Fludd finally dropped back to where he could watch the whole push.

He knew what he was up against.

This was a hardcase crew. Wasn't a ranny in the outfit that didn't have it in for him or that would hesitate, if a chance come along, to slip a slug between his ribs. What had happened to the old woman had nothing to do with it—or the fix the girl was in. Fludd knew what was eating them, and had known ever since he'd turned his gun on Jock Meyers. It was sheer damned envy. They couldn't stand to see somebody tougher than they were. They were burned up, that's what. It was eating them out to see how he'd gotten the jump on this spread.

It was Fludd's game every turn of the cards. And it wasn't just luck; it was his because he knew how to make it his. The girl would come round; she had no choice. But he would have to be up on his toes with the rest of them, have to watch every time he come near them—that, or give up the cattle.

Fludd rode with a rifle across the slant of his thighs.

*　　*　　*

Tara hadn't much choice as long as she was tied.

Fludd's ropes, however, had no hold on her thoughts, and for the first couple of hours of that interminable ride she employed her mind with schemes for making her range boss wish he'd never been born. But as her fury dropped into a kind of banked smolder and her physical discomfort became more painfully acute, she began to realize some of the things she'd refused to see.

Pearce, for instance. His quiet strength had been a rock she could never fall back on again.

The man had tried patiently to curb her reckless folly, and had given his life in that desperate attempt to get her free of the trap her pride and willfulness had sprung. Her eyes filled. But she would not let Fludd see her in tears! She was beginning to discover so many things that her stubbornness and arrogance had prevented her from seeing.

She had thought it absurd when her mother had said Star Circle was a millstone hung about her grandfather's neck, but now she could feel the awful weight of it. She had laughed at Pearce, scorning his counsel, despising the compassion she had glimpsed in his face—so bitterly resenting his attempts to guide and help her. 'Oh, Pearce...' she whispered in a choking voice. How blind she had been!

She had no thought for the passing miles, for the drop of sun behind distant crags, or the mutter of sullen talk flowing round her. When they finally stopped and the piggin string was untied from her ankles, Fludd roughly pulled her out of the saddle. She went down in a heap, unable to stand.

Fludd showed his contempt. 'Stay put,' he growled, and went stomping off.

Her ankles were puffed, and there was no feeling in them, but the scald of her wrists where the hemp still cut into them burned like hot wire.

Overwhelmed with nervous exhaustion, she

lay where she'd fallen, indifferent to the activity being carried on about her as the crew threw off saddles and took their horses to water, afterward staking them out for the night. A small fire gleamed in the lee of a boulder. The cook became busy with his pots and pans.

Now her legs nearly drove Tara crazy as restored circulation began to pump blood painfully through them. It seemed as though every bone in her body had been splintered with the pounding of that awful ride, every muscle stretched like a fiddle string, every sinew hobbled. She hadn't dreamed so much misery could descend on one person, but she embraced it, glad in this new-found spirit of contrition to endure whatever sorrows God in His anger might send her way.

In this mood of determined repentance she refused the supper one of the men brought over, relishing her distress with the satisfaction of a martyr. But this fervor did not long sustain her once the fire was out and the wind's increasing ferocity began to send the crew, shivering and cursing, into what shelter they were lucky enough to find. But even when she was almost frozen, she would not call out.

They were on the lease—she knew that much, deep into the Reservation. She had thought for a while that they must surely be discovered. But when hour followed hour, that hope finally faded; Indians had more sense than to be out in this kind of weather.

She wondered how long it actually took a person to freeze. Her arms were numb; even the pain in her legs didn't bother her now; a queer lassitude began to steal over her. The gale, she thought, must have blown itself out. She was no longer conscious of the cold in her bones. She smiled into the unseeing blackness, strangely secure with Pearce's arms wrapped about her...

And then he was shaking her. She felt the sting of his hand on her cheeks, and cried out. He kept cuffing her, roughly; she guessed he was shouting. He was hurting her now with all that jerking and slapping and, suddenly angered, she pried open her eyes to find Fludd crouched above her in the swirling shadows of a night grown unbelievably wild.

His voice came to her through the yammer of the wind. 'Get up outa that!' He shook her furiously. 'Don't think you're goin' to die on me!' Fludd cuffed her again. He hauled her to her feet. Two of the crew came out of the murk, and he shoved her at them. 'Walk some life back into her! Then get her on a horse!'

During all the black hours that were left, Tara rode with the crew through the howling gale, searching out and finding huddled masses of cattle piled against the wire, driving them away from it, not into the teeth of the wind but across it, picking up more, sweeping the lease fence clean of all that were able to respond to

186

the swinging ropes and continuous cursing. It was lucky for Fludd that Mike had put up that section of fence, or he never would have got the cattle at all. The crew scraped them up, prodding them along through the brush toward Star Circle.

It began to snow just before day broke, tiny round pellets that beat into them like hail.

Tara's wrists were free so that she might guide her mount, but her ankles were lashed again under its belly. She was too miserable to hope of getting away, too beaten to think; she could only feel as her horse floundered on in the wake of the increasing hundreds of bawling, horn-clacking cattle.

An hour after daylight the snow was still coming down, but the wind had fallen. They'd combed the whole west fence and were pointing south, trying to get the gather pushed off the lease before Chalkchild's Apaches should discover what they were up to. They were slowed to a shuffling, almost staggering walk. The horses were in bad shape, and the cows kept wanting to stop.

Fludd came up to where she rode in the drag. 'Push 'em, God damn it—let's git 'em to hell outa here!'

The men commenced popping their ropes again, standing up in their stirrups, waving their hats. 'Hyar-r-r! Hup! Hup!' they shouted, but the girl could see they weren't far from open rebellion.

She guessed Fludd saw it, too.

He dropped back a few lengths. When a commotion of twisting shaped up ahead and faint shouts drifted back, the natural thing would be for Fludd to ride up there. Though he hiked up his rifle, jacking a cartridge into the chamber, he didn't push forward.

Presently a rider came through the curtain of snow, keeping well out from the line of moving cattle. With his eyes cutting over the group in the drag, he drifted past without comment. He was one of the small owners who had a place east of Globe. She heard him hail Fludd. 'That bunch from More Oaks has moved in on you, mister. I came by yesterday mornin'. They're all over that range you run 'em outa last week. Facts is, they're clear on south—got their families, too. Looks like they're figgerin' on stayin'.'

Fludd didn't say anything. Tara looked back at him, stopping her horse. The men around her stopped, too.

There was a dark flush on the cheeks above Fludd's snow-whitened shoulders. The other man said: 'Somethin' else you mightn't know. They got signs up all over More Oaks—some in Stroud, tellin' them grangers Star Circle's free range, sayin' your spread's plumb open fer homesteadin'.'

'You son of a bitch!' Fludd said, and tipped up his rifle. In that falling snow the sound seemed hardly louder than a cough, but it

188

carried the other man over his cantle, knocking him flat across the hips of his horse. The horse bowed up, and tried, snorting, to dislodge him.

Tara saw the man come down. One of his boots got hung up in the stirrup. The horse took off, frantically kicking. Just after it faded in the thickening flakes, she thought she dimly heard a lifting chorus of shouts.

Her face whipped to Fludd.

His mouth was pulled back above the hunched, bony shoulders, the roan splotching of freckles standing out like wet paint. Someone called from afar. Someone else answered. A splutter of shots came out of the snow just beyond the stopped herd, and Fludd, his lips white with hatred, got hold of the girl's reins and, cursing, drove the men toward it.

Some pressure off to the left or the increased racket of continued firing had infected the cattle. In a contagion of fear the whole mass began moving, twisting away, bawling, breaking suddenly into a lumbering run that went tearing off into the heart of the lease.

The five hands with Fludd whirled their horses to head them. Fludd shouted and swore, but they sank spurs, and kept going. Tara, hoping to get clear in the confusion and turmoil, spun her own horse away from Fludd, slipping its bridle.

She heard the metallic sound of the rifle mechanism as the man threw another shell into the chamber. She flung both arms about the neck of her horse. Someone back of them shouted. There was a volley of shots.

Tara, peering back, saw Fludd crumpling groundward ... saw the wave of blue shapes coming up through the snow. Everywhere she looked there seemed to be more of them. Cavalrymen! Troopers! She shut her eyes hard, but the men in blue were still there when she opened them. She felt her horse stumble to a stop.

Here was the end of it. When the U.S. Army moved in, you were done. She was glad it was over so suddenly. She had regrets, of course; she couldn't help being sorry for many things, and she was frightened, too. But her defiance was gone, gone with the ignorance and hateful vanities that had bred it.

Sighing she turned, ready to accept whatever punishment she had to. A pair of troopers had the front of her horse wedged between them. But she hardly noticed them in the tremendous astonishment with which, her eyes enormous, she stared incredulously at the man just straightening from freeing her ankles.

Though she saw the bandage, she still couldn't believe it. But when he stretched up his arms and she fell tumbling into them, all she could say was: 'Now we can go! Now we can get away from the place—oh, *Pearce*!'

The strong arms folded her close.

Nelson Nye was born in Chicago, Illinois. He was educated in schools in Ohio and Massachusetts and attended the Cincinnati Art Academy. His early journalism experience was writing publicity releases and book reviews for the *Cincinnati Times-Star* and the *Buffalo Evening News*. In 1935 he began working as a ranch hand in Texas and California and became an expert on breeding quarter horses on his own ranch outside Tucson, Arizona. Much of this love for horses can be found in exceptional novels such as WILD HORSE SHORTY and BLOOD OF KINGS. He published his first Western short story in THRILLING WESTERN and his first Western novel in 1936. He continued from then on to write prolifically, both under his own name and the bylines Drake C. Denver and Clem Colt. During the Second World War, he served with the U.S. Army Field Artillery. In 1949–1952 he worked as horse editor for TEXAS LIVESTOCK JOURNAL. He was one of the founding members of the Western Writers of America in 1953 and served twice as its president. His first Golden Spur Award from the Western Writers of America came to him for best Western reviewer and critic in 1954. In 1958–1962 he was frontier fiction reviewer for the *New York Times Book Review*. His second Golden Spur came for his novel LONG RUN. His virtues as an author of Western fiction include a tremendous sense of authenticity, an ability to keep the pace of a story from ever lagging, and a fecund inventiveness for plot twists and situations. Some of his finest novels have had off-trail protagonists such as THE BARBER OF TUBAC and both NOT GRASS ALONE and STRAWBERRY ROAN are notable for their outstanding female characters. His books have sold over 50,000,000 copies worldwide and have been translated into the principal European languages. The *Los Angeles Times* once praised him for his 'marvelous lingo, salty humor, and real characters.' Above all, a Nye Western possesses a vital energy that is both propulsive and persuasive.

We hope you have enjoyed this Large Print book. Other Chivers Press or G. K. Hall Large Print books are available at your library or directly from the publishers. For more information about current and forthcoming titles, please call or write, without obligation, to:

Chivers Press Limited
Windsor Bridge Road
Bath BA2 3AX
England
Tel. (01225) 335336

OR

G. K. Hall
P.O. Box 159
Thorndike, Maine 04986
USA
Tel. (800) 223–6121 (U.S. & Canada)
In Maine call collect: (207) 948–2962

All our Large Print titles are designed for easy reading, and all our books are made to last.

OCT 2 3 1997			
MAR 1 4			